1

Jenny

I first met Sam Horsfall on the beach at Brighton. And it's all very well for my father to raise his eyebrows, but it was because of him that it happened. I mean, any ordinary parent with a reasonable income and an only daughter would buy that daughter a camera when she asked for it, and just be glad if she only wanted a cheap one. But my father isn't an ordinary parent; well, not ordinary *enough*. He's an architect with a big practice. He designs town centres and sits on committees and gives lectures. My mother says he has exceptional qualities that are bound to spill over into his private life. I expect she's right, really, but the overspill can be hard to live with.

That's how it was the morning I asked for a camera.

'They cost far too much,' Father said, lowering his newspaper nearly into the marmalade and looking at me severely over the top of it.

'I don't want an expensive one. Just one like Susan's.'

'And what is Susan's like?'

'Well, it's not a great square heavy thing you look into the top of, like yours. It's little, and you look at it through one eye. She gets good snaps; she's got a nice album full of prints of where she's been.'

'How does it focus?'

'Oh, *I* don't know, Da. It looks the same shape roughly as Uncle Dick's.'

'A Leica. She only wants a Leica,' my father said to my mother. And to me, 'You'll have to wait till next birthday. *And* be lucky.'

'Perhaps if you got that contract for the industrial estate . . .' said my mother, who is always optimistic and usually on my side.

'For heaven's sake, Emily!' cried my father. 'A decent camera costs hundreds of pounds!'

'Oh, Da, I don't *want* one that costs hundreds of pounds! I just want an ordinary plain cheap one like anyone else would have, like Susan's got, or Mary, and that costs ten pounds, about. Please.'

'I often wonder, Emily,' said my father weightily, shaking that handsome head of his, 'exactly how we have failed our daughter. As obviously we have done. If there is one thing above another in my own personal culture that I would wish to transmit to my child, it would be a care for quality and an understanding of the value of the *best*, a dislike of all things shoddy. I simply cannot understand how a child of mine could want a cheap camera!'

'Oh, *Da!*' I said, exasperated, but seeing all too clearly that I wasn't going to get a snazzy little camera like Susan's.

'I'll tell you what, Jenny,' my father said. He sounded as if he was relenting, but I've known him too long to be taken in. 'You can borrow mine.'

'Yours weighs a *ton*, Da, and it's ever so difficult . . .'

'Borrow mine and learn to use it properly. Bring me some really good work taken with mine, and then if you still want a cheap camera I'll buy you one with no more questions asked. *If* you still want one.'

'Wouldn't it be safer if I learned on something less valuable than yours? What if I had an accident? What if I broke it?'

'It's insured,' my father said. 'But don't.'

And just for once Gramp wasn't sympathetic either. He and Gran live in a little house five miles away, in a modest part of Richmond-on-Thames called the Alberts. I love them both, and I go there for tea most Wednesdays after school.

'You won't get anywhere with one of those,' Gramp said

6

when I described Susan's camera. 'Why don't you borrow your father's? Thank your lucky stars you have the chance.'

So I borrowed the wretched thing.

Susan was not impressed. 'Trust *you*, Jenny Midhurst,' she said sarcastically when I met her at the station, 'to have some awful great thing like that. We're going to look like ruddy sightseers from a mile off.'

'Well, we *are* sightseeing, aren't we? What do people go to Brighton *for*?'

Susan sniffed. She really was quite cross. Her camera was in her Greek shoulder-bag, beside her lunch. Mine was rather conspicuous, festooned around my neck, all in ginger-coloured leather. All the same, as we got into the train, I wondered just what had annoyed her. After all, we were going on a trip to Brighton, and we were going specially to take snapshots, because of all the snaps she had taken last summer on her family's southcoast tour, only the ones at Brighton hadn't come out. The point was to replace the Brighton shots in her album and to start *my* album. I liked hers, and I wanted one too.

'Can't you ever be like a normal person?' she asked, as the train drew away from the platform. She eyed my offending camera balefully as it sat in the luggage rack. 'And those sandals you're wearing!' she added. 'Trust you!'

By now I was looking out of the window and feeling quite happy. I didn't say what I thought, which was that she was going to break her ankles wearing platform shoes on a shingle beach, if she wasn't careful.

Susan and I had become friends because we both started at our present school in mid-year, when everyone else had got themselves fixed up already. I suppose we considered ourselves to be best friends. But we didn't really have a lot in common. Susan thought I was the class freak, forever going around in a dream; and maybe she had a point. I admit it was just like me to be wearing those rather childish sandals, which I'd put on without thinking about it. It wasn't that I *wanted* to be different. I've always tried quite hard to be like other people, but somehow I don't seem to manage it.

And as I sat in the train I was thinking that although I wanted an album I didn't want one like Susan's. She had people and places in hers: what my Gramp always called the 'Auntie-at-the-Eiffel-Tower' school. What I wanted was something she had got by accident once or twice: an actual frozen moment, the light and shade and feel of a single instant in time. If you could collect those moments, I was thinking, if you could put your personal impression on them and tuck them away for ever between the leaves of an album, you'd have stopped the world and won a little bit of it for yourself . . .

The Brighton day didn't work.

I was very patient at first. We walked around a good deal, and ate ice-cream and drank Cokes. I gazed open-mouthed and delighted at the Pavilion, but I was careful not to suggest going inside, because Susan would have been bored to the backbone.

I did think we might take some pictures of it, though. And right away there were snags. Susan agreed, whipped out her camera, lined it up and clicked. Done. Finished. Then she got very cross waiting for me. First, I took longer than she had done choosing a view. Then, Dad's camera has to be focused very carefully, looking down through the top and twiddling a knob on the side, and then you have to use a light meter to work out the exposure, and then set the exposure on the camera. Dad had shown me, but I wasn't used to it, and I did take rather a long time.

Susan stood around, tapping her shoe loudly on the pavement and tutting audibly, which didn't help my concentration. I didn't know why she was fussing. I'd have thought she'd be quite all right, just watching the world go by. I'm not so green that I hadn't noticed how eyeing any boys we happened to pass was most of the point of being there anyway, so far as she was concerned.

But she got very agitated, and began to carry on at me about hurrying up and getting along somewhere else, as though it really mattered. When I finally took my picture I was a bit flustered and didn't know whether I'd done it right or not.

'For heaven's sake, come *on!*' Susan hissed in a stage whisper.

'What's the matter?'

'Don't look now. There's someone staring at us.'

'Oh, really?' I said. 'Might be staring at *you*, maybe. I never have any trouble when I'm by myself.'

'I bet you don't!' said Susan sarcastically. 'But he was gawking at you more than me. Must be a weirdo. Come on, let's go somewhere else!'

'Let's go to the beach, then.'

'The *beach*? Why the beach? It's all stones.'

'I want to take a picture of the sea,' I said. 'I haven't come all this way to miss the sea.'

'Oh, all right. Anything, as long as we move. But I'm not going on the beach; I'll stay on the promenade.'

That was all right by me. I left her there.

I like the beach at Brighton. I like being down there under the cliff, half-way out to sea. There's a dramatic row of fine houses, far above, overlooking you, and on this particular day the afternoon light was picking them out and making them glow, like an old print. The roadway is two-tier, on elegant cast-iron arches, and then there's the pier, reaching out over the water, all lacy and decorative in silhouette against the sky. And the sea, lazy and placid (though it isn't always like that), toying with the beach but not troubling to assert itself; just playing its endless game of piling pebbles. I wanted to take a picture of those pebbles. Just pebbles, lying.

Susan wouldn't risk her shoes on the shingle, so she stayed leaning over the railings in a carefully careless attitude. To keep her happy, I started by photographing her. Then I took the pier, and then the tall cliff with the row of houses. Long before I had finished fiddling with the focus and exposure for that shot, Susan was sending a piercing whisper in my direction.

'Jenny! Look! I mean, *don't* look! It's him! He's here! That boy! He's followed us!'

I went on focusing the camera.

'Come on, Jen!' she called, loudly this time. 'Let's get away from here!'

'I've got one more picture to take,' I said. And I shut my ears to her nagging, and concentrated on getting a reach of stones in the view-finder just as I wanted it, with nothing else in the picture by accident. Susan climbed down on the beach and clattered and slithered precariously over to me, as though we needed to stand together against attack.

'Oh, do come *along*, Jen!' she urged me.

'What's the fuss?' I asked. 'We're on a public beach, close by the promenade. Nobody's going to assault us. Anyway, *you* don't usually run away from boys!' I nearly added, 'Quite the reverse!' but just managed to stop myself.

'I don't like the look of *him*!' said Susan. 'Of course, it's you he's staring at, but he can see you're with me.'

'He can now,' I said drily. 'Now, if you were to take one step to the left, I could take this picture without your foot in it.' But as Susan's feet disappeared from the view-finder, a pair of rather battered men's brogues appeared in it from the other direction. That was my first encounter with Sam Horsfall: standing where he wasn't wanted, right in the middle of my picture.

I looked up scowling, to see a round-faced young man with bright brown eyes and a diffident expression; with dark hair all over the place and no tie and elbows patched with leather.

'Go away!' said Susan beside me.

'I want to ask you something!' said this character. I didn't know then that he was Sam, of course, but I knew at once from the way he said it that he was from the North.

10

'The answer's no,' said Susan. 'No, whatever you had in mind. No, we don't want a cup of coffee, we don't want to walk, we don't want to be shown round Brighton, we don't want male company at all. So shove off!'

The young man looked at me. His expression was rather desperate. 'I wanted to ask,' he said, 'if I could borrow that camera for a while. Please.'

'Bloody cheek!' said Susan. 'Say no, Jenny. It's only a blind. It's you he's after, really.'

'I'm not!' said the Sam character, furiously. 'I'm only interested in the camera!' And then he blushed bright pink and said 'Sorry, I didn't mean that. I meant . . . Well, I meant, I *need* the camera.'

'You are the rudest person I've met in a long time!' Susan told him. She was still cross, but I was trying to stop giggling.

'I'm sorry,' I said when I'd got myself under control, 'but I can't possibly lend it. It's valuable and it isn't mine.'

'Please!' said the Sam character. 'You wouldn't have to let it out of your sight for an instant. Please don't say no without letting me tell you about it.'

'All right,' I said. 'Just let me finish taking this picture, and then you can have three minutes to tell me everything. And it had better be good.'

And it was good; very good. Susan didn't believe him, or said she didn't, but I believed him, and I let him use the camera. I patiently trudged around after him, not letting it out of my sight. Susan soon detached herself, towards a group of young men outside a coffee-bar, and promised to meet me at the station. I was very impressed by the way Sam handled the camera, but not all that impressed by what he chose to point it at.

When all the film was used up, he took it out of the camera and pocketed it. He promised to send me free prints of my shots, in return for the ones he'd used. I gave him my address on a piece of paper, and went off to catch the train. I was rather cold and bored with standing around; I could have done with a cup of coffee, but he didn't offer.

Susan arrived at the last minute, just as I was wondering whether I'd have to miss the train and hang around some more. When we were settled in the carriage and the train was pulling out, she asked if Sam had got me into a quiet corner and made a pass at me. She seemed disappointed, almost affronted, when I told her he hadn't.

'He's got a bloody nerve, just exploiting you like that!' she said. But if he *had* made a pass at me, I thought, she'd have been just as indignant. She said I'd never see or hear of my film again, especially when I admitted that I hadn't got his address. I didn't ask what had happened to *her* after we separated, but she told me all the way home anyway.

I wasn't worried about my film. I'd decided that although Sam might have some rough edges he seemed quite a straight-forward, honest sort of person. I confidently expected some prints of Brighton to turn up in the post a day or two later.

2

Sam

It's not like me to lose things. Where I come from, you're careful with possessions. You have to be. The first thing you learn is that everything costs money and money doesn't grow on trees. Of course, there are some at the Polytechnic who act as if it was all easy-come-easy-go, and maybe it *is*, if you come from a well-off family. But I don't pretend to come from a well-off family. In fact I don't pretend at all. Plain speaking's what I believe in, and facing up to things as they are. We're good at facing facts in the North. We stop believing in Father Christmas before we can talk.

The stuff I lost had cost a packet; about as much as I get in grant for a whole year, at a guess. It belonged to the Poly, and I'd had to sign for it. So it was a right mess when I saw that car disappear round the corner, with all my gear inside it. And with it, to all appearances, went my chance of winning the competition and getting a trial with the local rag, because it was a sure bet that the Poly wouldn't let me borrow anything else until the year 2084, and it would take me about as long as that to save up enough to buy the equipment for myself. In a split second I could see my whole future collapsing, like a Yorkshire pudding made in the South.

And if it hadn't been for the girl, I reckon it would have done. I really did want to win that competition and that job. And I'll admit — being frank by nature — I'll admit that I wanted to show them all at home what I can do. Because my friends and family back in Bradford aren't going to be all that impressed by my B.A. degree in Visual Studies, if I ever get it. I can just hear my Uncle Jack asking, 'What the hell are Visual Studies?' and my Uncle Herbert saying, 'Taking nude photos, I expect,' and Uncle Jack saying, 'Nice work if you can get it, eh?', and both of them sniggering. But they'd be impressed if I went back north and said I'd won this competition and got a job lined up. They'd understand that all right. They might even think it had been worth while going to Barhampton Polytechnic instead of leaving school and looking for work.

The competition was Larry Lomas's idea. Larry is the lecturer-in-charge of photography, which is my special subject. He's twenty-seven, which is young for a teacher in a polytechnic, and he's the low man on the totem-pole. In fact he's more like one of us than one of them, if by them you mean the high-ups at the Poly. Larry comes under the Head of Graphic Arts, who comes under the Dean of Visual Studies, who comes under the Deputy Director for Art and Design, who comes under the Director of the whole enormous Polytechnic, which has about a big enough population to apply for membership of the United Nations.

Larry is a good bloke, although he has a lot of fancy ideas about photography as an art that I don't go along with, being very practical myself. (Where I come from, we have to be practical.) He'll take a lot of trouble for you, and if he knows you're hard up he'll manage to get materials for you out of the college stores, although really you're supposed to buy film and printing paper for yourself.

Well, every year since the year dot the Poly has produced a calendar with a large picture on it, to send out to important people. The picture was always a painting by one of the Fine Arts students until last year, when one of the important people who receive the calendar asked the Director what the picture was a picture *of*, and the Director couldn't tell him. So the Director asked the

Deputy Director for Art and Design what it was a picture of, and the Deputy Director asked the Dean of Visual Studies, and the Dean of Visual Studies asked the Head of Graphic Art, and the Head of Graphic Art asked the student. And the message passed back up the chain of command was that the picture wasn't *of* anything; it just *was*.

Whereupon the Director said he thought it was time the Photography Department contributed the calendar picture for a change.

So the Director told the Deputy Director, and the Deputy Director told the Dean of Visual Studies, and the Dean of Visual Studies told the Head of Graphic Art, and the Head of Graphic Art told Larry. Larry was delighted, because this was what he'd been rooting for without success ever since he came to the Poly. And he got the high-ups to agree that there should be a competition, open to all the photography students — that's me and about forty other chaps and girls — to be judged by a panel consisting of the Director, the department heads in Art and Design and the editor-in-chief of our evening paper, the *Barhampton Echo*, whose picture editor is a pal of Larry's.

The winning entry would appear on the calendar. There would be a small cash prize, with even smaller cash prizes for the entries placed second and third. And there was the prospect of a more important reward. Larry had heard from the picture editor that old Tom Sigsworth, who had been one of the *Echo's* three staff photographers since about 1066, was due to retire next year. And Larry did a deal with his pal to the effect that — subject to the editor-in-chief's approval — he would give a three-month trial to whoever won the competition. And if this person did well on trial, he or she would be accepted as Graduate Entry and put through the proper training scheme and become a fully-fledged newspaper photographer.

Well, it was hedged about a bit, but it sounded a pretty fair offer to me. It was a better job than most of us in the department would dare to hope for. Industrial photography was about the best we could expect after we graduated. Or, failing that, a job as a demonstrator or technician. Or a salesman in a camera shop, which was a fate worse than death. Or, of course, the dole.

So I wanted like hell to win. I thought I had a good chance, too. The title of the competition was 'The Eye of the Beholder', and it would be judged a few days before the end of the autumn term, which had just begun. Most of our lot would put in some kind of entry, but they wouldn't spend too much time and trouble on it, because either they weren't that keen on a newspaper job or they reckoned they had enough to do in completing their assignments for their course. I was sure that if I really took the trouble and put in a top-class job I could beat them all. The only person I saw as a serious rival was a girl called Elaine Anders, a fancy bit of goods from Cheltenham, who always seems to have all the lads after her. I don't think much of Elaine's work myself, but I'll admit frankly that she can take photographs that some people like. There's no accounting for tastes. And I knew she really wanted that newspaper job. Well, it has to be something glamorous for that kind of girl, and next to television I suppose she thought newspapers were the best thing going.

I'd worked out my approach to this competition. I knew that a lot of our group would put in clever-clever pictures, the sort of thing where you don't know whether it's sunset in Sherwood Forest or a set of false teeth for a shark. But I reckoned that after last year's experience with the Fine Arts the Director wouldn't fancy that kind of effort. And I knew that all the faculty people in Art and Design, including Larry, keep going on about the inter-relatedness of the Arts and all that. So I decided that what would be right up everybody's street would be a beautiful picture of a beautiful building. Or, of course, a row or group of beautiful buildings. It would be a marriage of two arts, so to speak, photography and architecture. It would please the Director, because if anybody asked what it was, he'd be able to tell them. And with reasonable luck it would win the vote of the Dean of Architecture, who'd be on the judging panel.

I must admit there was a bit of low cunning involved in this calculation. I don't really approve of low cunning; we don't go in for it much in Bradford; but there are times when even the highest standards have to be relaxed a bit, and one of these times is when it's a matter of getting a job. I knew just where I was going to start looking for my subject. Brighton. Where better to look for beautiful buildings than Brighton?

The other thing I'd decided was that my picture was going to be technically superb. An immaculate print from an immaculate negative. Nobody would be able to fault it on that ground. Because I reckoned this was where I had the edge on Elaine Anders. The only work of hers I'd seen that looked out of the ordinary was rather romantic and fuzzy. It was womanish stuff in fact, if you'll forgive me for appearing to be a male chauvinist, which I'm not, having always been a strong believer in women's rights, so long as they don't start getting above themselves. I was remembering that the editor-in-chief of the *Echo* would be one of the judges, and I was sure a newspaper editor would prefer good clean work, the sort that would reproduce well in half-tone.

Now for really good architectural photography you have to think big — at least a two-and-a-quarter-inch negative, in my opinion. And good large-format cameras cost a bomb. I don't have the kind of money involved. I have just one camera, and it's a 35-millimetre Pentax, four years old. It cost me £50 secondhand, and I had enough trouble raising the money for that. Luckily I have digs with my Auntie Edith, who came to Barhampton from Bradford ten years ago and charges me less than I'd pay anywhere else, so I manage, but there's nothing to spare for fancy equipment.

But there's one good thing about the Poly, and that is

that they'll lend you equipment, provided you have a
genuine need for it, which I had, and provided you've a
clean record of bringing back what you borrowed before,
which I had up to that time. So I set off bright and early
this fine September morning to hitch to Brighton. I had
a tripod under my arm, and I had a pack on my back with
the Poly's best Hasselblad camera and a light meter and
spare lenses and other oddments, as well as my lunch and
my raincoat. All the gear was expensive. I'd never been
worth as much in my life. I got round west and southwest
London easily enough in a couple of hitches, and
eveything was all right until I arrived at the A24 at
Dorking. And there I stuck. And stuck. And it got hot.
For September it got very hot. I got hot with it. It isn't
easy to keep cool when you're all dressed up like a
Christmas tree.

I have a theory about getting rides. The Horsfall Theory
of Hitching. It doesn't apply to dishy-looking girls, of
course. They get them quickly enough. But for the rest
of us the chance of getting a quick lift is in inverse propor-
tion to the degree to which you look as if you need one.
If you wore a hat and a beautiful black coat and striped
pants and carried a rolled umbrella and a copy of the
Financial Times, you'd have cars queueing up to offer you
a lift. But look like a shabby, hard-up student and they'll
accelerate past you.

Well, a shabby, hard-up student was what I looked like.
And was. And I waited near Dorking for what seemed like
half a morning before the chap came along in the green
Cavalier and stopped for me without hesitation and was
really nice and friendly. He was a commercial traveller.
I slung my stuff in the back and we got talking, and I told
him what I thought about politics and sex and religion and
education and a few other subjects, and it was all very
pleasant.

As I say, I'm not forgetful. In fact I didn't exactly
forget. It was just that when I got out of the car my head
was full of what I'd been saying, and it was a second or

two before it sank in that I'd better be opening the back door and getting my stuff out. And by the time it registered, this absent-minded fellow was driving away. He wasn't stealing my gear, there's no question of that. He was just a bit careless. Some folk are like that.

He'd taken everything, even my sandwiches.

I jumped into the roadway and yelled after him, but of course he didn't hear, and all I achieved was to make two or three passers-by look uneasy, as if they didn't know whether I was drunk or had escaped from a mental institution. My next idea was to stay where I was, in the hope that he'd realize before long what had happened and would come back looking for me. I still think that was a sensible plan, but it didn't work. I spent the next hour standing on the pavement feeling hot outside and hollow inside, and wondering what Larry would say to me and what the Head of Graphic Arts would say to *him*, and forever thinking I could see the Cavalier coming back and then realizing it wasn't.

At the end of that hour I did my sums and calculated that if the man reappeared now it would mean he'd driven at least twenty miles back to me, which was too much to expect. So my third and last thought was to go and tell the story at the police station, which I did. They took my address, and they suggested that it might be worth my while to stay around for the rest of the day and call in again before I went home. This was because there was a chance that the chap might be coming back the same way in the normal course of business, in which case he'd most likely take the stuff in to the Brighton police.

Well, that made sense of course, and it also meant I'd better stay in Brighton until early evening. So at half-past two there I was, with nothing to do and nowhere to go and an empty belly and seventeen pence in my pocket. And all the cares of the world on my shoulders, or so it seemed to me.

I say I had nothing to do, but I had to do something, and I felt it would at least keep me occupied and take my mind off my troubles if I were to walk round and decide what pictures I would take if and when I did get the equipment back.

And that's what I was doing when I saw the girl. Or rather, to be accurate, when I saw the two girls, because she had a pal with her at that stage. Or rather, to be more accurate still, that was when I saw the camera. The camera startled me because it was a Hasselblad, the twin brother of the one I'd left in the car.

For a wild moment I thought it was the same camera, that had in some magical way jumped out of the man's car and got itself down to Brighton beach. Of course, it couldn't be. The girl's carrying-case was different, anyway. But it tortured me to see it. It was a *real* camera, a professional's camera, a camera for a person who knew just what he was doing.

And did this girl know what she was doing? Not on your nelly. Mind you, she was making quite a performance of it. She was in front of the Pavilion, which is big and obvious enough, and she walked this way and she walked that way and then she walked forward and then she walked back until she was practically in the traffic. And when I thought she'd made up her mind, it turned out she hadn't, and she started the whole performance again. At last she found her spot, and then she spent centuries focusing the thing, and enough time for half a dozen ice ages to come and go while she peered at the light meter.

If I'd been in a mood to be amused, I'd have had fun just watching the other girl while all this went on. I knew *her* type right away. Ordinary all-purpose teenage girl, current production-line model. Sole interests, boys and clothes and pop. Or maybe boys and pop and clothes. Boys first, anyway. And when a girl like that is at a place like Brighton with a girlfriend, I know just what she has in mind. She hopes they'll get off with a couple of boys, and she'll have the good-looking one.

This girl was fidgeting and tapping her foot and looking at her watch and frowning fit to crack a lens. Then she saw me, and kept staring at me with a minus quantity of enthusiasm. I could tell she didn't fancy me, and anyway what good is one boy between two girls? Then she started whispering to the camera girl and looking across at me between times, and I knew it was me she was whispering about and it wasn't complimentary. And then they both set off for the beach. The camera girl hadn't even looked at me, but the other one turned round once or twice and glared at me over her shoulder and made more comments to her friend.

The girl with the camera wasn't taking much notice. She went on the beach, slipping and skidding on the pebbles, and took a picture of her friend and one of the pier and one of the cliff. The friend meanwhile stayed on the promenade, scowling. I went up and leaned on the railings a few yards away from her, and this made her scowl even more fiercely and hiss at the camera girl, 'Jenny! Look! He's followed us!'

So that was her name. Jenny. I was studying her with a bit of interest now. It was quite true that I'd followed them, or at any rate that I'd followed the camera. I'd been struck by the wild hope that I could borrow it and take my pictures anyway. And I was wondering whether Jenny was the sort of person you could borrow a camera from.

Actually I quite liked the look of her. Medium height, slight-to-medium build. Big, serious eyes. Hair straight and light-brown, parted in the middle, early-Victorian style. Nice complexion and a good bone structure. I wouldn't have minded doing a studio portrait of her. You'd never make her look pretty, but there was something about that face that you could bring out a treat with the right lighting. The other girl was more attractive at first sight: dark and a bit on the plump side, with a bold eye and plenty of vitality. But at a second glance you'd think — well, if you were me you'd think she wasn't really worth a second glance.

'Let's get out of here!' she called now to her friend, giving me another dirty look, and then she was on the beach and the two of them were arguing, and then Jenny was setting up shop to take a picture of pebbles. Just pebbles. A million pebbles, and every one of them pretty much the same as the other 999,999. Not my idea of a picture at all. She must have been hard-pressed for something to take, I thought.

But I still liked the look of her. And I liked the way she wasn't giving in to the other girl. So I took a deep breath and stepped in front of her and asked her the key question. Could I borrow her camera for a while?

I knew it was cheek, and if I hadn't known it was cheek the other girl would soon have made it clear. She was pretty scathing, and I was embarrassed, and Jenny giggled, and it was all rather awful. Then Jenny hummed and hawed a bit and said the camera was valuable and wasn't hers and all that, but I got the impression that she wasn't actually dead set against letting me use it. So I offered to explain and she gave me three minutes to do it in. And I did. I told her straight what had happened. 'I expect it sounds unlikely,' I said, 'but it's true. Honestly it is.'

'I believe you,' she said.

'Oh, do you?' said the other girl, nastily.

'This is Susan,' the camera girl said. 'I'm Jenny.'

'I'm Sam.'

'Hello, Sam,' said Jenny. But Susan just sniffed, and looked at me as if I was something smelly the tide had washed up.

'I think I ought to let Sam use my dad's camera,' Jenny said. 'Don't you, Sue?'

'Frankly, no,' said Susan.

'After all, it's his future, isn't it?' Jenny said. 'Besides, I might pick up a few hints on how to do it.'

Then I knew I'd won, and so did Susan, and she didn't like me any the better for it. Jenny handed the camera over, and off we went. I tried to be friendly to Susan, but it went against the grain, because I didn't take to her any more than she did to me. In fact there was an atmosphere between us that you could have cut with a blunt pair of scissors. Before long, Susan dropped behind, sulking. Soon after we'd left the beach we passed a coffee-bar, and a group of lads whistled and made cheeky remarks about her, and Susan made remarks back, and in about one minute flat she'd peeled away from us and attached herself to them, with nothing said except a casual promise to Jenny to meet her at the station.

'I'm sorry about that,' I said.

'Oh, it doesn't matter.'

'I didn't mean to come between you and your friend.'

'Well, you haven't, not really. I mean, Susan and I were both a bit fed up with each other today, but it won't make any difference, we'll be friends again by the time we get home.'

So we went round Brighton together, and I took more pictures of the Pavilion, and some of the pier, and some of a rather handsome Regency terrace on the cliff top called Tamarisk Walk, and some of the Lanes, which are a warren of alleyways full of book and antique shops that Jenny thought were picturesque. I'll admit that I did rather want Jenny to think I was an expert, and I handled that camera with a casual air that certainly impressed her, though I'm afraid as a result I wasn't as careful as I should have been.

When the film was finished, I took it out of the camera and promised to develop it at the Poly, and I said I'd send her the negatives and free prints of all her pictures. She seemed quite happy with that arrangement. So she wrote her name and address on a bit of paper, which I shoved in my pocket along with the film. I'd have taken her for a cup of coffee, but I hadn't enough money, and after the favour she'd done me I didn't like the idea of her having to go Dutch. And fortunately she said it was time she went for her train. So I said, 'Good-bye, Jenny,' and she said, 'Good-bye, Sam,' and I said, 'See you sometime, I hope,' but I didn't think for a minute I ever would. She lived at Kingston, on the Surrey side of London, and I never go to Kingston. Not that I'd have minded seeing her again. I'd quite liked her, though I'd jump over a cliff to get away from that Susan.

I went to the police station then. The same constable was at the desk as before, and he just shook his head at me. He promised they'd get in touch if ever they heard anything, but he didn't sound too hopeful and I went out feeling full of gloom.

And I had one hell of a time getting back to Barhampton. You'd think the Horsfall Theory of Hitching had suddenly been given the force of law. Nobody wanted my company. I was over an hour getting out of Brighton, and then I was stuck twice more. It was midnight and I was practically dropping with hunger when I rolled in at Auntie Edith's. They'd gone to bed but she came down in her dressing-gown and gave me a sandwich and a large piece of her mind.

The next day I developed the film, and blow me if my pictures weren't all duds. I'd made a gross mistake about the speed of the film. Infuriatingly, Jenny's weren't bad at all. Even the shot of horrible Susan had something — you could tell exactly what kind of girl she was, simply from her posture as she leaned against the railings. And the picture of all the pebbles was arty and ridiculous, but if you wanted a picture of a lot of pebbles, well I suppose it was a pretty good picture of a lot of pebbles.

I made nice big prints of them all, and wrote a little note to go with them. And then, just to round off the whole chapter of accidents, I found I'd lost Jenny's address. I ransacked my pockets for that bit of paper, but no luck. The annoying thing is that it's not like me to lose anything. I'm not one of these casual folk that have had it easy all their lives and don't care if they lose something because they can always buy more. Where I come from, we take care of things. But it must have been my unlucky day. And as I'd put the paper in my pocket without really looking at it, I couldn't remember her address or even her surname. There wasn't much hope of tracking her down with nothing to go on but the fact that she was called Jenny and came from Kingston.

I'd told her I was at Barhampton Polytechnic, so it was possible that she'd get in touch with me. I hoped she would. But perhaps she'd think I wasn't going to bother and wouldn't do anything about it. Either way it was embarrassing.

I put the packet of prints in my locker and, pretty down-hearted by now, went off to break the news about the camera to Larry Lomas.

3

Jenny

The prints didn't come and didn't come, and after a while I got quite annoyed. Not that I really wanted them; I'd rather gone off the idea of compiling a photo album, which was clearly going to be more trouble than it was worth. But I did want to be proved right in having trusted Sam Horsfall. By letting me down he was making me seem a fool.

Of course, I was being got at by Susan. Every morning she'd pounce on me the moment I arrived at school, asking, 'Have they come yet?' And she got more and more gleeful every time they hadn't. Not content with triumphant 'What-did-I-tell-yous', she had told all the others about this awful boy who had taken me in with a ridiculous story, had an afternoon's free use of my camera, and then walked off with the film. Some of them made pitying remarks about my innocence and some gave me the kind of smirking sympathy that's ten times worse than none at all. I'd soon had enough of this, and I longed for the prints to come, because of course I would only have to wave them around to put an end to the ribbing.

But however long you allow for waiting for a turn in the darkroom and making and drying prints and the various hitches Sam had told me about, to say nothing of delays in the post, it couldn't take three weeks for them to arrive, if they were ever going to. So in the end I had to admit, even to myself, that it looked as if I'd been conned.

I was quite a bit angry, but gloomy even more than

angry, so that Gramp noticed and asked me why. I was at Gran's and Gramp's house for tea. Gramp is small and wiry and cheerful and Gran is small and soft and cheerful. Gramp likes to talk to me about Life and Literature, and he goes on about Plato and Newton and Keats and Shelley. Gran likes to feed me up, and she makes bridge rolls and scones and treacle tart. And we all like to do the newspaper crossword together, sitting round a coal fire when it gets to be autumn, as it was doing now.

I couldn't make anything of the crossword that day, and got called Clueless Kate by Gran, which was a dreadful pun. Then Gramp asked what was the matter, and I told him. I could see at once he thought it was a bit rash of me to have lent the camera.

'Well, at least the Hasselblad didn't come to any harm,' he said consolingly when I'd finished.

'Yes, but he ought to have sent me my prints. He said he would.'

'I expect he meant to,' said Gramp. 'But people are a bit casual these days.'

'I know, it was different when *you* were young,' I said. And then, 'Dammit, it's not just a matter of being casual. What it boils down to is that he hoodwinked me and stole my film!'

'Now why do you think she minds?' said Gramp to Gran. And to me, 'Was he nice-looking, this young chap?'

'No, he wasn't!' I said crossly. 'He was moon-faced, and he was wearing horrible clothes, and he had an accent like somebody in one of those kitchen-sink plays on telly. Not my type at all!'

'Got round you for the camera, though, didn't he?' said Gramp, grinning.

'Well it was the hard-luck story that did that, I expect,' said Gran. 'You know our Jenny.'

I had an odd feeling that my remarks had been unfair and disloyal to Sam, though of course I didn't owe him any loyalty.

'He just seemed like somebody you could trust,' I said.

'Well, perhaps he is, dear,' said Gran. 'Perhaps he just lost your address.'

'Lost the address?' said Gramp. 'Some folk will believe anything.'

Gran ignored that. 'Could *you* get in touch with *him*, dear?' she suggested.

I frowned. I hadn't meant to do any such thing. But . . .

'Come on, we're neglecting the crossword,' said Gramp. 'What about "Are you acquainted with a lady in northern Italy?" Five letters. Blank, E, blank, blank, blank.'

'Genoa,' I said. 'Give me another.'

When I thought it over at home later, I felt quite cheered by Gran's idea. It was worth a try. I knew he was called Sam. I knew he was at Barhampton Polytechnic. I knew he was doing Visual Studies. That ought to be enough. I would write to him.

I hesitated for a long time over what to say. A postcard, I decided, would be better than a letter. The message would be brief. The tone would be wry and mocking and rather sophisticated. And after a good deal of drafting and crossing-out on bits of paper, I arrived at what I thought was a suitable text:

> Oh, Sam! Sam! I trusted
> you! I gave you what you
> wanted! Have you broken
> faith with
> > your
> > Jenny?

I addressed the card to 'Sam, Visual Studies Dept., The Polytechnic, Barhampton.' I posted it. And I tried to take no notice of Susan.

4

Sam

I'd always thought Larry Lomas liked me. In fact I still
think he does. But you wouldn't have guessed it from the
way he looked and spoke that Monday morning when I
told him about the lost gear. I suppose I was a bit daft
to break it to him on a wet Monday, straight after the
weekly faculty meeting, which Larry had to go to, and
which always left him a bit frayed round the edges. I
could have let it wait two or three days, in the hope of
getting news of the stuff before anyone started asking
awkward questions. But that's not my style. I had to own
up at once. The information was kind of burning a hole
in my head and needing to get out.

'You absolute incredible bloody fool, Sam Horsfall!'
Larry said. 'You mean to say you left all this valuable
equipment in the back of somebody's car and just watched
him drive away? And didn't even get the car number?'

'I was thinking about the conversation we'd just had,'
I told him.

'A fascinating subject, no doubt,' said Larry sarcastically 'My God, I wouldn't think much of that as an excuse
if it came from a kid of twelve!'

That hurt, and his next remark hurt even more.

'You know what, Sam?' he said. 'You make yourself out
to be a hard-headed Yorkshireman, and the truth is,
you're a soft-headed twit.' And then, very cross and letting his metaphors get out of control, he went on, 'And
if you don't get your head out of the clouds and your feet
on the ground, you're going to come unstuck!'

By now I'd shrunk from my usual five foot ten to about two and half inches. Larry went on, more quietly but still cutting: 'And you *would* choose a time when the budget's been cut to the bone and we've just had the D.D.' (that's the Deputy Director) 'going on at us about waste and carelessness. And here are you, doing a damnfool thing like this. And it isn't even *old* equipment, it's the newest and most expensive we've got. It's insured for theft or accident, but not for being left lying around by half-witted students.'

'I expect we'll get it back,' I said.

'Let's hope so,' said Larry. 'You realize that, if we don't, under the rules of the Polytechnic you have to pay for it?'

'And how much will that be?'

'Can't say off-hand. At least a thousand pounds.'

'Where do you think I'd find a thousand pounds?' I asked.

Larry sighed deeply and shook his head.

'You can't,' he said. 'Therefore, we write it off. Therefore I get a rollicking from the D.D., if not from the Director himself. Therefore also, other students who could have used the stuff are disappointed. Honestly, Sam, I don't know what God was thinking about when He created *you*. And listen, do you know you could be refused your degree for having an unpaid debt to the Poly? That's in the statutes. I don't suppose the Director would apply it, but he could if he felt so inclined.'

He sighed again.

'Do what you can, Sam,' he said. 'Keep in touch with the police. And you said this man was a commercial traveller? Well, there's a commercial travellers' association. I expect they have a journal. See if you can put a small ad in it, or write a letter to the editor or something. And the best of British luck to you. And until or unless we get the stuff back, you don't borrow anything else, understand? And now, bugger off out of here before I get *really* cross!'

It wasn't exactly a pleasant interview. I didn't say much

about it to the other students. But news of these things gets around. That afternoon Elaine Anders came up to me with a voice as sweet as saccharine.

'If you've finished what you're doing, Sam,' she said, 'why don't we go round the corner for a cup of tea?'

'Me? With you?' I said.

'Yes. That was the idea.'

'What do you want?'

'Sam!' she said. It was a protesting voice, but there was a giggle lurking behind it, and it irritated me. 'I don't want anything but your company, Sam. And I'm inviting you. I shall pay with my own pennies.'

That irritated me still more.

'I'm not going to be paid for by you!' I said.

'All right, then,' Her voice was still sweet. 'If you have to be sexist about it, you can pay with *your* pennies.'

'But *I* haven't invited *you*.'

She didn't say anything, and I thought that had shut her up. Then I realized that her lips were pressed hard together and she was trying not to laugh.

'Oh, to hell with it!' I said. 'All right, then, let's go. You can pay if you like. I suppose it all comes from Daddy anyway, and he can afford it.'

'What I like about you, Sam,' she said, 'is your unfailing charm.'

That was a silly remark. We don't go in for charm much, up our way. But I let it pass. I waited while she went for her coat. Then we walked round the corner to Pam's Pantry. Actually there's a cafeteria in the Poly, and the prices are much lower than Pam's, but the cafeteria is where you all go in a bunch, with general conversation and lots of backchat. Pam's is where you go when you have something to say in private.

Elaine was clutching an envelope, the kind you put prints in. I kept looking at it and wondering what she was up to. I'd known Elaine for over a year and we hadn't had a lot to do with each other. To be frank about it (and I believe in being frank) I wouldn't have thought I was her type any more than she was mine. She was a pretty girl, in a way that hadn't been much in fashion lately. She wore sweaters and jeans, because that was what girls did wear at the Poly, but she'd have looked better in a dinky little frock that showed off her slim waist and nice legs. She had blue eyes and red-blonde curly hair, and her face was powdered with sexy little freckles. And she had a tiny, light, high, precise voice that was pure Cheltenham, and a tinkly, affected laugh. At least, it always sounded affected to me. I suppose it was natural to her.

But she wasn't a dumb blonde. Oh, no. No way. She was a formidable character, and I didn't underrate her. She managed most of the fellows like a puppeteer managing marionettes. Just a jerk of her little finger and they danced to her tune.

Now she was looking at me sympathetically across the table.

'You look as if you were having a rough time, Sam,' she said.

'Yes. That's because I'm having a rough time.'

'Trouble with Larry?'

'Yes. I expect you know what it's about.'

'I did hear something. Hard luck, Sam.'

She put a little cool hand on mine, which was resting on the table. I was startled. Also I realized I needed sympathy. Anybody's. Even hers. I found myself putting my other hand on top of hers, making a hand sandwich. It surprised me more than it did her. She asked me all over again how the loss of the gear had happened, and what I was doing about it, and when she said she hoped it would be all right in the end I almost started liking her.

Then she took her hand out from between mine and said, 'Can I ask you a favour, Sam? Tell me what you think of these.' And she pulled some prints out of that envelope. I was surprised, because we're all showing each other prints all the time. You don't usually go round to Pam's Pantry to show somebody some prints.

They were fancy, rather trendy stuff, the sort you might

have seen in a glossy magazine. Interesting to a photographer for technical reasons. There were deliberately grainy prints, and deliberately hard and low-tone prints, and prints that were outrageously contrasty, and prints so spooky that they didn't look as if they could have reached the paper by normal chemical processes at all. They were obviously made by a darkroom wizard of a fairly high order. Some of them showed girls from the Poly, with less clothes on than I'd ever seen them in, and some showed sophisticated interiors with pot-plants and drinks on trays, advertising-agency style; but there were also outdoor shots of pavements and brick walls and roofs, chosen for their patterns and textures. I have to admit I was quite impressed.

'You made these?' I asked.

'Uh-huh.'

'Very clever. Why are you showing them to me?'

'I wondered what you thought of them, that's all.'

'They're good. But why ask me rather than anyone else?'

'I wanted somebody whose judgement I could trust.' A flattering little smile. 'You see, Sam, I don't want them seen by all and sundry. I'm thinking of putting some of them in for the calendar competition.'

I looked at her rather hard. She looked back at me with innocent blue eyes. Carefully innocent.

'Listen, Elaine,' I said. 'I'm going in for that contest too.'

She seemed surprised. 'You are?' she said. 'Seriously?'

'I'm dead serious,' I told her.

'I hadn't thought it was quite in your line, somehow,' she said.

'Why not?'

'Oh, I don't know. I'd have thought it might call for more . . . Well, never mind.' The light, high little voice quickened. 'It seems we're rivals, then.'

She put out her hand again and shook mine, in the formal, slightly comic way that people do on these occasions. And then she didn't take the hand away. 'Oh,

33

well,' she said, 'may the best man win. Or woman, as the case may be.'

And I had the sense that she was confident. Very confident. I thought of my under-exposed pictures of Brighton Pier and Pavilion. No good at all. You could find much better ones on any old postcard. I'd have to improve on them a thousand per cent if I was to have any chance of beating Elaine. I'd got the right idea, I thought, but I'd blundered in carrying it out. If only the missing camera would turn up. Or if I could borrow Jenny's again — but that seemed impossible, seeing I'd lost her address. I felt gloom slowly pouring over me from the top of the head down, like a kind of grey treacle. I didn't want to sit there with Elaine any more. I drew my hand away from hers.

'Well,' I said, 'hadn't you better be paying the bill?'

She didn't like that: the drawing back I mean. Chaps don't usually draw back from Elaine. Quite the reverse. They come on as fast as she'll let them. There was an icy look in those guileless blue eyes. We walked back to the Poly together, but we didn't say much, and she didn't take my hand again.

Later that afternoon, when everybody but me had gone, Larry came out of his poky little office.

'Cheer up, Sam,' he said. 'It'll all be the same in a hundred years' time. Sorry I had to give you such a roasting, though you must admit you deserved it. I'm going to have a quick pint of ale on my way home. Care to join me?'

I declined with thanks. I hadn't any money for buying pints, and I don't like not standing my round. But Larry didn't dash off immediately. His mood seemed to have lightened since the morning. He was more like his usual self — that is, like a friend who worked alongside us rather than an official representative of the Poly.

'I saw you go out and come back with Elaine this afternoon,' he remarked.

'Oh?' I tried to put a that's-my-business tone into my voice, but Larry wasn't sensitive to it.

'What if she fancies you?' he said.

'Me? Don't be daft, Larry. Anyway, she goes out with Tim Weldon.'

'Used to,' said Larry. 'Doesn't now. That broke up. You might catch her on the rebound. If you wanted to, of course.'

I'll admit I felt a bit flattered that Larry thought it possible. There was hardly a chap in the department who wouldn't have liked to think that Elaine Anders fancied him.

'I gather she's going in for the calendar competition,' I said.

'I wouldn't be surprised.'

'Is she likely to win it, Larry?'

Larry frowned.

'No comment on that,' he said. 'I know she's been busy lately, but I haven't seen any of the results. I told you all at the start, there are two things I'm not doing. I'm not looking at your prospective entries and I'm not giving you any advice. You've got to work it out for yourselves.'

'She must be a strong candidate, though,' I said.

'Well, yes. I don't give anything away by agreeing with you there. I'd say Elaine's a very strong candidate. She has something vital that so many of us lack. She has imagination. The visual imagination.'

'And I haven't?' I said, wondering if that was what Elaine had almost told me earlier in the afternoon. Larry appeared not to hear, and hurried away in search of his pint. Between them, he and Elaine and the man in the Cavalier had got me gloomed up enough to last for a fortnight. And when that card of Jenny's appeared on the notice-board, it didn't exactly leave me rolling helpless with laughter all over the corridor.

Actually that was three weeks later. And it was pretty rotten of the Post Room at the Poly to stick it up on the notice-board like that. It was addressed to 'Sam' at the Visual Studies Department, and there isn't any other Sam in the Department. Even if the Post Room didn't know that, they could easily have found out — a word to the Head of Deparment's secretary would have been enough — and then they could have put it in my pigeon-hole and nobody else would have seen it. But no, some lout in the Post Room had read it, thought it was good for a giggle, and put it up on our board among the notices about club meetings and concerts and switching off lights and not leaving bicycles unlocked.

There was a whole gang of people standing round the board when I arrived that morning, all with silly grins on their faces. They made way for me, and just in case I didn't see the card, Ian Burns asked, 'Is there anyone called Sam around here?' I went up and read it, and I knew at once who it was from. She wanted to know what had happened to her prints, which was fair enough, but she'd worded the card so that it sounded as if I'd been having it off with some girl somewhere and walked away from her, probably leaving her pregnant at that. Anyway, that's how the mob around the notice-board were taking it, and they were going to have their fun. Jenny hadn't realized what infantile minds some students have.

I whipped the card from the board and shoved it in my pocket, but I could feel my cheeks going red as I did so. 'Oh, is it for *you*?' Ian Burns asked, wide-eyed, with a clottish attempt to look innocent. Somebody asked if I'd enjoyed it and somebody else wanted to know if they could have the next turn and sombody else again said I was a rotten bastard to treat a girl like that, and although all these remarks were facetious they didn't amuse me at all. And bloody Elain Anders, with her guileless look and little-girl voice, said primly, 'Will somebody tell me the joke?', which made them all roar again, because nobody thinks you can tell Elaine much.

So I just stalked grimly away, with my face still red; and fortunately I had a lecture immediately afterwards and then some work I could do in the library, so I didn't need to go into the Department that day. And by the following day my card was on the way to being forgotten, though there were still a few grins when I appeared, and as a matter of fact a vulgar postcard has been called 'a Sam' in our Department ever since, though I bet very few people now know where the term came from.

Not that Jenny's was a vulgar postcard, of course, but it was certainly an embarrassing one. I was a bit upset about the notice-board episode, and cross with her for letting me in for being laughed at; and at the same time I was a bit indignant on her behalf. In a curious kind of way I felt she was being smeared.

At least she'd put her address on the card, so now at last I could do as I'd promised. I took out the envelope that had been in my locker for the last three weeks, with her prints in it. I put in a note that said. 'Thanks for card. Sorry about delay. Lost your address. Will be in touch.' And I put it in the post, first-class, which always causes a pang, postal charges being what they are, but I didn't want her to have another day of thinking I'd let her down.

I'll admit that her camera was still very much in my mind. In the three weeks that had passed, I'd done everything I could think of, and there'd been no result whatever. The last time I'd telephoned Brighton police — on Larry's office phone, with his permission — they'd told me rather wearily that there was still no news, and assured me that they'd contact me if they ever heard anything. I had a feeling that what they were really saying was that it was no use bothering them any more.

I'd decided what I wanted to do about the competition. What was wrong with Brighton was that it was too smart and seasidey. No real old-England thatched atmosphere, if you know what I mean. Over the three weeks I'd toyed with the thought of trying again in one place or another, and eventually I'd had a brainwave. I was going to marry art and architecture. Why not literature as well? That would *really* be inter-cultural. The high-ups would love it.

And what were the big names in literature? Well, I hadn't done much of that for a few years but I'm not so ignorant that I don't know a few of the names. What bigger name than W. Shakespeare? And Shakespeare suggested Stratford-on-Avon, and Stratford was a real genuine old-world town. Eureka. Couldn't miss. All I needed was the camera. And now that I'd heard from Jenny it began at last to seem as if the camera might be available. So, after three weeks of being down, my spirits were rising a bit when I went home to tea that day at Auntie Edith's.

I might have known. Along with the Horsfall Theory of Hitching, my contribution to modern thought includes Horsfall's Law of Sheer Cussedness. And as soon as I began to cheer up, it came crashing into operation.

You must have encountered Horsfall's Law, though maybe you know it under some other name. Horsfall's Law says that if you arrive early to catch a train, the train will be late, but if you arrive late the train will have left on time. Horsfall's Law says that if there's just one book missing from the library shelf, it will be the one you want. Horsfall's Law says that if you lose something and you put off replacing it because of the cost, but eventually you decide that you've just *got* to replace it, then the day after you've paid for a new one the old one will turn up.

It was a variation on this last clause of Horsfall's Law that I tripped over. For three weeks I hadn't had Jenny's address. But the very day her card arrived, the original bit of paper was found. It was Auntie Edith who found it. It would be.

Auntie Edith is my mum's sister. She moved from Bradford to Barhampton ten years ago, when Uncle Frank got a job there, but her heart's still in Bradford and will be until the day she dies. When I got a place at Barhampton Poly, Mum and Auntie were overjoyed, and Auntie said right away that I could live with her for just the cost of my food. That was a good offer, because the price of lodgings in Barhampton is enough to frighten an oil sheikh. 'Your Auntie Edith's house will be just like home,' Mum said; and so it is. That's what's wrong with it. It's a bit more posh than Solomon Street: in fact it's semi-detached; but the atmosphere is the same.

It's not that I object too much to Monday being washday come hell or high water, or to taking off my shoes before I tread on the sitting-room carpet. Or even to conversation being mainly on such topics as whether meat is a penny a pound cheaper at Tesco than at the local butcher's. It's the inquisitiveness. Auntie Edith's greatest interest in life is in what other people are up to, and her greatest satisfaction lies in finding out, in the fullest possible detail.

Uncle Frank doesn't give her much scope, because she knows exactly what *he* does, and it never changes from one year's end to the next. On weekdays he goes to work, comes home, has his tea and watches telly. On Saturdays and Sundays he goes fishing in the canal. That's it. Neighbours are more interesting, but also frustrating, because you don't get to know them in a Barhampton suburb the way you would in a Bradford street. So to have a nephew of student age staying with her was as near as Auntie Edith could expect to get to having her dreams come true. She could strip people of their secrets as quickly and neatly as shelling peas. I didn't actually have many secrets, but I did need to have a bit of life of my own, and it was a non-stop struggle.

She found the scrap of paper in the old jacket I wore to go to Brighton. Somehow or other I'd managed to push it through a tear in the lining instead of into my pocket. Auntie Edith discovered it while trying to extract a twopenny piece that had also fallen through the lining. And trust her to tell me about it the moment I got home.

'Jenny Midhurst,' she read from it. 'The Pines, Spinney Lane, Kingston, Surry. Telephone Kingston 927. A young lady, eh?' She was delighted. 'You're a dark horse, aren't you, Sam Horsfall? Never said anything about *her*, did you?'

'There's nothing to say.'

'Oh, no? How did you meet her? Kingston's a long way from here.' Auntie pondered, then pounced on the solution like a detective in a play. '*I* can guess. That day you said you were going to Brighton and came back so late. That was the day you met this young lady. Am I right, Sam? Am I right?'

She wagged a roguish finger at me. I said nothing.

'She writes a nice hand, anyway,' Auntie remarked.

I ought to have had the sense to go on saying nothing. There was so little to go on that even Auntie would soon have exhausted the possibilities of the subject. But I was really irritated. First the notice-board incident, then this.

'Listen, Auntie,' I said. 'Can't you mind your own business, just for once?'

Well, then the balloon went up. You've no idea how hurt my auntie can be. I won't spell it out, but she gave me the whole works. Here she was, all these years in this strange town and still hardly knew anybody, and Uncle Frank so quiet and nobody to talk to or think about but her own family, and didn't mean any harm and only taking an interest and might as well not be here at all . . .

In the end I had to put my arms round her and comfort her and apologize over and over again and tell her what there was to tell about Jenny, which actually wasn't much. She asked a great many questions about Jenny's home, parents, brothers, sisters, pets, clothes, school and circumstances in general, hardly any of which I could answer. The fact that I obviously didn't know Jenny very well didn't bother her, though. She soon got quite romantic, and thought it would be just the thing for me to have a nice little girl-friend, and if she was still at school, well, so much the better. Some of these girl students weren't all they should be, if what she'd been told was true. A pity though, that Kingston was so far. Did I have any plans for seeing Jenny again?

Well, actually I *was* beginning to think I wouldn't mind spending another day with Jenny, though not for the reasons Auntie Edith supposed. Auntie didn't understand the attractions of a Hasselblad. And it wasn't *only* the camera. I was feeling a bit fed up with Barhampton and the Poly and Larry and Elaine and the notice-board sniggerers and Auntie Edith and Uncle Frank — everything and everybody — and the thought of a day away from them all was an appealing one. And I was still quite excited by the Stratford idea. A day at Stratford, perhaps . . .

'I might,' I said, 'I just *might* suggest going out for the day on Saturday or Sunday, if she could manage it and wanted to.'

'Oh, yes!' said Auntie Edith eagerly. She was positively starry-eyed about it. 'Well, dear, you have a telephone number for her. Why don't you ring her now? Strike while the iron's hot, so to speak. Go and telephone her while I make your meal. Jenny. Yes, I like it as a name. A bit old-fashioned, but nothing wrong with that. Jenny . . .'

I wouldn't have dared to close the door between her and the room where the telephone was.

5

Jenny

There must be something in this telepathy business. In spite of his three-week silence I knew when the phone rang that it would be him. I think it was the way it rang just at the very moment when I was walking past it, as if it was reaching out and catching me by the sleeve. And of course I recognized those flat northern tones at once.

'Can I speak to Jenny, please?'

'Speaking.'

'Well, it's Sam here. Sam Horsfall. You met me at Brighton. Remember?'

I didn't intend to sound too enthusiastic. Not after all that time.

'Oh, yes, I remember,' I said in a mildly surprised tone, as if I'd managed with an effort to sort him out from all the other Sams in my life. 'You're the one who borrowed my camera and walked off with the film.'

'I'm sorry about that. I lost the address.'

'But you got my postcard?'

'Yes. And your prints are on the way. In the post. They're not so bad, some of them — better than I thought they'd be. You could do it quite well if you really tried.'

'Oh, thank you. Thank you *so* much!' But sarcasm was wasted on Sam Horsfall.

'That's nothing,' he said. 'You're welcome.'

'So what can I do for you now?'

'Well, I, er, wondered if you'd like to come and take some more pictures somewhere else. What I had in mind

42

was Shakespeare's place — Stratford-on-Avon. Do you know Stratford?'

'Yes, I do, actually. Quite well.'

'Oh. Then would you fancy a day there?'

'I don't know. I might . . . You've got your camera back, then?'

'No, actually I haven't. Not yet. I was hoping you'd bring your dad's again. Will you?'

So *that* was what it was about. I might have known.

'You've got a nerve, Sam Horsfall, haven't you?'

'Well, you see, it's like this.' And he launched into an explanation of his difficulties and how good the Hasselblad was and how helpful I'd been and how I could help him again if I felt like it. It wasn't exactly a masterpiece of tact. Plenty about the camera and about Sam and the problems of Sam, and an honourable mention for my helpfulness, but nothing about liking my company. Not a speech designed to get the best results. But I must be the softest touch going. By the time he'd finished, I was promising to meet him at the Stratford bus station next Saturday at noon.

I promised without even knowing for sure that I could have the camera on Saturday. After I'd hung up, I tried to imagine what Sam would say if I turned up without it. Would he be polite and forgiving? I didn't think so. He'd be more likely to say, 'If you'd let me know in time we needn't have come!'

I asked my father about it in the drawing-room after supper. He was sitting in his favourite armchair with a sheaf of papers on his knee. My mother was there as well.

Dad was quite willing that I should have the Hasselblad again. He seemed pleased that I wanted it. I expect he saw it as a sign of success in his efforts to keep me from the temptations of cheap cameras, and by implication all the other cheap things of life. Mother was less interested in the camera than in where I was going, and with whom.

'Stratford-on-Avon?' she said. 'Is it a school trip, Jen? You never told me about one.'

'It isn't a school trip,' I said.

'You're going with Susan, then?'

'No,' I said.

'You're not going to Stratford on your *own*, Jenny, are you?' my mother asked. I knew her tone of voice. It carried an unspoken comment: 'That's just the kind of peculiar thing you *would* do.'

'No, I'm not,' I said. 'I'm meeting somebody.'

I waited for the next question, but it didn't come. My parents have progressive views on not intruding into my life, though my mother is sometimes a bit wistful about it. I think she would like to have more mother-and-daughter heart-to-hearts than we ever manage to have.

Anyway, there was an awkward silence, and I left the room, intending to go and do some homework. Then I remembered I hadn't thanked my father for agreeing to let me have the camera. I pushed the door open, to come back in again. And I heard my mother's voice saying clearly and with conviction. 'She's going to meet a boy!' And my father, not really attending, ' A what? Oh, a boy. I see.'

I marched into the middle of the room and said, 'I will now make an announcement. I am going to Stratford-upon-Avon with a young man. His name is Sam Horsfall. I first met him at Brighton three weeks ago. Are there any questions?'

My mother said, 'Really, Jenny! There's no need to be like that!' But she was smiling. I can read her like a Beginner Book. She was delighted that I was doing something normal, such as anybody else's teenage daughter might do.

'I'd better *not* ask any questions, had I?' she said. 'I might be told to mind my own business.' She looked at me expectantly, all the same.

I knew what she would want to know first about Sam. His occupation.

'He's a student,' I said.

That was all right. A satisfied maternal smile.

'At Barhampton Polytechnic,' I added.

44

That wasn't quite so all right. To my mother, the word 'student' meant a university student, preferably at Oxford or Cambridge. But my father looked up from his sheaf of papers and asked, shortly, 'What subject?'

'Photography.'

'Hence the request for the camera,' said my father. 'He shows discrimination. I hope he's teaching you to use it.'

He looked down at the papers again.

'I don't know him *well*,' I said. 'It isn't *serious*. He's just somebody I met. I'm helping him with a project.'

'Tell us about it, Jen dear,' my mother invited. She was still bright-eyed. But my father looked up again.

'It's Jenny's life,' he said, 'Don't interrogate her. She'll tell us what she wants us to know.'

My mother subsided, squashed. It must be tough for her sometimes, living with Dad and me. I don't behave the way she thinks of as normal, and Dad doesn't know what the word 'normal' means. He just behaves like himself, regardless of anyone else.

'However,' my father went on, addressing me, 'if you're going to keep on seeing this young man, I'd be glad if you'd bring him home one of these days. I'd like to see who's got his hands on my Hasselblad.'

That's my father all over. He asks who's after his camera, not who's after his daughter. He asks it in a dry, humorous tone, of course, and it doesn't really mean he cares more about the camera than about me. It's because of me that he's interested in meeting Sam. But he wouldn't ever claim a right to inspect his daughter's friends. He owns the camera, he doesn't own *me*, and when he says a thing like that it's his way of admitting it. It's why, although he's impossible sometimes, I actually *like* him . . .

I wish I could see myself as clearly as I see him.

I went up to my own room, where I was supposed to be doing that homework, and sat in the window-seat. It's a bay window that juts out almost into the branches of an apple tree. I hadn't drawn the curtains, and the ceiling light in my bedroom was reflected so that it looked as if there was a parallel light out there somewhere in the middle of the tree.

It was October now, and the tree had shed most of its leaves and fruit. There were just a few small, scruffy, much-pecked apples hanging on in a dejected kind of way. Spring would come of course, and the tree would break leaf again with that soft milky green of tender freshness that always made me light-headed with excitement; but just now it was the dying end of the year. Why had I agreed to go to Stratford at this time, when I didn't even much like the place? Sometimes, I thought, I baffle me completely.

Of course, it could be just kindness. Here was poor Sam without a camera, and here was I with one, and it would be an act of humanity, typical of my nature as I sometimes tried to imagine it. My life would be like that, a long vista of selflessness: my hand always ready to soothe the fevered brow, my door open to everyone, my wealth, if any, at the disposal of all who needed it. If not actually a saint, I would be a Florence Nightingale . . . But at that point, my power to daydream gave out. I might not know much about myself, but I knew I wasn't *that* virtuous.

Why, then, go to Stratford with Sam? If it wasn't kindness, perhaps it was liking? Maybe this was one of those supposedly delicious outbreaks of feeling for one particular boy that afflicted the rest of my form whenever they could find any occasion for it. I tried to imagine myself hand-in-hand with Sam, leaning tenderly against him while he put his arms round me; but I just couldn't. I not only couldn't imagine what it might feel like to be clasped to the breast of Sam Horsfall; I didn't *want* to imagine it. I recalled with relief that he couldn't put his arms round me or anyone else without first putting down all his gear and this would allow time to run. But, *really!* How could I suppose Sam would make a pass at me? I was nothing to him but a device for supplying him with

46

a camera, and if he found the one he'd lost he wouldn't need me any more.

So, why . . .?

Perhaps it was actually the photography that appealed? After all, it was through photography that we'd met in the first place, and Sam now said I could be good at it if I really tried. Maybe it was the challenge and excitement of the competition. Or maybe it was Sam's personal problems that interested me as a student of human nature. (I liked that phrase. Surely I was a student of human nature, and probably a rather talented one.) Sam needed to get himself together, to stop losing things, to learn to disguise his intentions just enough to be socially acceptable . . .

Oh, come off it, Jenny! I told myself in the end, disgusted. Come off it! The truth was, I wasn't specially interested either in a trip to Stratford or in Sam. I wasn't under any obligation to lend him the camera. I could easily ring him back and invent a forgotten date or a parental veto, and that would be the end of the matter.

Why go to Stratford with Sam? Why indeed? I'd explored all the possible reasons and not one of them had convinced me. But I knew I would go just the same.

Next morning my prints arrived. Sam had done his best with them. They were huge, glossy affairs, looking very grand. I flipped through them eagerly. There was the Pavilion, there was the row of cliff-top houses, there was the pier in fine sharp outline — quite a good one, that — and there was Susan leaning on the railings. And there was the picture of pebbles only.

I looked at them all again more closely; and when the impression of splendour given by sheer size had worn off my spirits sank a shade. I decided they weren't really all that exciting. Pavilion, pier, cliff-top cottages — they were just *views*. They could have been picture postcards, except that postcards always have lurid sunlight in them, as if the scene in question had been transplanted to the tropics. The pebble picture was all very well, but it didn't have either shape or content: it was rather drearily arty. Maybe it all went to prove that photography, like lots of other things, was harder than it looked.

Irritatingly, the best picture by far was the one of Susan against the railings. By accident, that one had caught the truth of Susan. She looked just what she was: a rather ordinary teenager in the pose of a fashion model; and, I thought cattily, she was displaying the differences — the curves of puppy-fat in place of the model's greyhound slimness, the ankles that were just a shade too thick. Thanks to the Hasselblad, you could even detect the spot on her cheek that she'd carefully covered up . . .

The prints were a wow at school, though. Even with Susan. When she saw the picture of herself, she recovered rapidly from her irritation at being proved wrong in predicting that Sam would never be heard of again. I suppose self-love must be blind, and that what Susan saw in the picture was the fashion model rather than the ordinary teenager. I generously gave her the print, and after all she'd said about Sam she had the cheek to ask if he could make some more for her. Other people were impressed by my pictures, too. I came in for quite a bit of praise and congratulation for the scenic stuff. Gloomily I reflected that the road to glory as the snapshot champion of the school was apparently to take very ordinary photographs and have them printed very large.

I took them with me to Wednesday tea with Gran and Gramp.

'Hmmm,' said Gramp. 'Whose work are these?'

'I took the pictures,' I said, 'and that Sam character I was telling you about made the prints.'

'There!' said Gran. 'I knew he wouldn't really have let you down. Has the poor boy found his camera, do you know?'

'He hadn't up to Monday night,' I said.

'Well, starting from the pictures you took,' said Gramp,

'I don't see how he could have done much better than these. Of course, everyone uses hard papers these days, not like when I was doing it.'

'You can make prints, Gramp?' I asked.

'Used to be quite keen, once,' he said. 'Hang on a minute.'

'Now what have you done?' said Gran, as he left the room and could be heard plodding up the stairs. 'We won't have time to do the crossword, now you've got him started.'

'Sorry, Gran,' I said, grinning.

Gramp came back with a big dusty brown folder. The tape that fastened it had rotted through, and broke when he tried to untie it. Inside were a lot of sepia pictures, all very pale.

'They've faded,' I said.

'No,' said Gramp. 'I wanted them like that. Went to a lot of trouble to get them just so.'

Gramp's landscapes all looked as if seen through a light mist. There were streets uncluttered by traffic, and views of cathedrals, all soft and grainy. A small pond reflected church and sky in its pale fawn surface. And there was a sequence of pictures of urchins in ragged clothes, some with no shoes.

'There was shocking poverty in those days,' said Gramp. 'I wanted to show it as it was.'

I wondered why I didn't feel shocked and horrified myself, then realized that the pictures had been transformed by time and didn't now suggest acutal poverty at all. Those children had faded into the past and had a kind of nostalgic charm, like the streets that were clear of cars and road signs.

The last picture was different from all the rest. It showed a beautiful young woman in profile, with dark heavy hair loosely braided down her back, long straight nose, long curved neck, and sweet serious expression on the lips.

'You know who that is?' asked Gramp.

I had a moment's doubt, and then I knew for sure. 'It's Gran!' I said. 'Oh Gran, you were beautiful!'

A second later I felt sorry I'd said that, in case she was wounded. But all she said was, 'I've still got that plait somewhere. I had my hair bobbed, but I kept the plait.'

Later that afternoon she showed it me: shiny, deep-chestnut hair, lying coiled in a drawer, with blue ribbon tied on each end. I was sad for a moment, and felt tears come to my eyes, but Gran was still quite matter-of-fact. Walking home afterwards, it occurred to me that although time had done strange things to Gramp's pictures, Gramp's pictures had still won out over time. True, those poor children had lost reality and become merely picturesque. But on the other hand, Gramp's photographs were all that could now show me Gran's young face or the light in which he himself had once seen the world.

It's funny stuff, time; as hard to understand as people, or art, or me.

6

Sam

She never lets go. I mean my Auntie Edith. Once she'd latched on to the fact that I was planning to spend a day at Stratford with *a young lady* (her italics), she wouldn't let the subject drop. She reminded me every hour on the hour, and usually a few times in between. If I hadn't shaved for a day or two, or I'd forgotten to brush my hair, or I was wearing that tatty old sweater that I like but that Auntie abominates, she'd tell me coyly that *that* wouldn't do for Jenny. She asked me the same questions about Jenny and her family again and again, even when I'd already told her I didn't know the answer. Whatever she put in front of me to eat, she inquired whether or not Jenny liked it.

'I don't *know* whether she likes pork sausages,' I'd say, or, 'I haven't *asked* her what she thinks about fish fingers.' Then Auntie would look hurt and say she was only showing interest. Too true she was. She tried to embroil Uncle Frank in these discussions, but he has brought not listening to Auntie to a fine art. He just goes on munching, or watching 'Coronation Street', and murmuring 'Yes, love' or 'No, love' at intervals. He knows from her voice which of these is required, and never gets it wrong. I'd have avoided coming in for meals at all, but what with not having been able to get a job last vacation, and starting the term under a load of debt, I was desperately short of money. I couldn't afford to eat out.

I couldn't afford to go to Stratford by coach, either, so I was planning to hitch again. Auntie cooked up a scheme for Uncle to take me in his car, with herself in the back seat, going 'just for the ride'. But mercifully Uncle had promised to go fishing with a couple of cronies a few miles down the canal in the other direction, and needed the car for that. In spite of numerous remarks by Auntie, he stuck by his intentions, with the silent stubbornness that's his main defence against her. So hitching it was.

When Saturday came, Auntie would have had me on the road at crack of dawn. 'You mustn't keep her waiting,' she told me. '*That's* not the way to treat a young lady.' But I knew that on a Saturday outside the holiday season it's no use trying to hitch too early in the morning. There was a battle of wills, in which the more she tried to hurry me the more I insisted there was lots of time. In the end I overdid my resistance and left it rather late. And as I might have guessed, by the operation of Horsfall's Law, I had a lot of trouble getting a ride and didn't reach Stratford until half an hour after Jenny's coach was due in.

The camera was there all right. It was in its leather case, sitting on her lap, on a bench in the coach station. She was behind it − just a girl in a raincoat; pale, slight, quite ordinary-looking. Younger than I'd remembered. But the big, wide eyes: I'd remembered those. A faraway look in them. In fact she was lost to her surroundings. She might have been a thousand miles away for all the notice she was taking of what went on around her. She hadn't even got the strap round her neck. Somebody could have snatched the Hasselblad and been away round a couple of corners before she knew what was happening.

I went up and planted myself in front of her. *Then* she saw me. She came back to earth and her eyes into focus and I thought she blushed, very slightly.

'Hello,' I said. 'Shall I carry the camera?'

'Hello,' she said. She got up and handed it over to me, and we stood for a moment looking at each other. It was just a shade awkward. The trouble was, I hadn't just got the camera for the day, I'd got the girl for the day as well. It struck me now that a girl was a responsibility, almost as much as a camera. She'd come all this way to help me, and I couldn't just leave her somewhere and forget about her. In fact I ought to do something to make her trip worth while. Like giving her a bit more tuition in photography.

Anyway, it was no good messing about. I was here on business, and I'd better get on with it. Jenny had said on the phone that she'd be expected home for supper, which would mean leaving Stratford by teatime. There'd been a couple of showers earlier on, and although the day now seemed to have turned fine, I didn't entirely trust it.

'Let's go,' I said. 'You know the town, don't you? Take me where the action is. I mean, Shakespeare's birthplace and all that.'

She gave me a funny, kind of sideways, look. Then she said, 'All right. This way.' And I must admit, she did know her way around Stratford.

It didn't take long to get to the birthplace, and it was quite satisfactory from a photographic point of view. Not thatched, but lots of half-timbering, and not too difficult to get a good angle on. I took a few shots from the street, and then we went into the garden and I took some more. I explained to Jenny about film speed and exposure and aperture. Then I thought perhaps it was only fair to let her have a go, seeing it was her own camera, or at any rate her old man's. She didn't seem all that keen, until a big cloud came over. Then she got excited and took two pictures, one after the other. I could see that one of them would have nothing of the birthplace in it but a chimney-stack, and the other wouldn't have any birthplace in it at all; only a bit of tree. But when I pointed this out to her, she said, 'I just liked the cloud.'

'Listen,' I said. 'There are clouds *everywhere* every day of the week. You don't have to come to Stratford to find a cloud!'

That shut her up.

There was a museum in the birthplace and a modern affair close by called the Shakespeare Centre, but I wasn't much interested in those. We walked through the streets and I took quite a lot of pictures. There were more and more half-timbered buildings, mostly with Shakespeare associations. I made notes as I went along, so I'd know which building was which and what the Bard did in them, like go to school. But when I told Jenny what I was doing, she said, 'Couldn't you get all that from a guide-book?' I didn't tell her that anything I spent on a guide-book would be that much less to spend on food.

We couldn't see the house Shakespeare retired to, because somebody had pulled it down two hundred years ago, but we went into his daughter's house, where she lived with her husband, who was a famous doctor. Jenny seemed more interested in this old doc's dispensary, with all its medical weirderies, than she had been in the Shakespeare stuff, which surprised me, because I'd got the impression that she was a poetic kind of person. She specially liked the old guy's contribution to medicine: 'Select Observations on English Bodies: or, Cures both Empiricall and Historicall, performed upon very eminent Persons in desperate Diseases.'

'What desperate disease have *you* got?' I said. 'And if you had one, do you think some old seventeenth-century quack would have the cure for it?'

That shut her up again.

'We haven't done too badly,' I said after a while. 'The one thing I haven't got so far is thatch. I thought Stratford would have been more thatched.'

'There's always Anne Hathaway's cottage,' she said.

We had to walk along a footpath to the cottage, which certainly had plenty of thatch, and a garden that was very pretty even at this time of year. But I knew I'd seen a picture of it before, and as soon as I set eyes on it I remembered. My other auntie, Auntie Elsie, has it on a tea-tray.

'I think maybe it's too familiar,' I said to Jenny.

'Is that possible?' she asked. There was a funny edge to her voice. For a moment I almost thought she was being sarcastic.

'Well, yes, it is,' I explained. 'It's probably been on lots of calendars already.'

'Oh,' she said, and then, 'Sam I'm tired and I'm getting hungry. Why don't we go and eat?'

'All right,' I said. I was feeling quite hungry myself. I'd noticed a fast-food joint out of the corner of my eye as we walked through the streets, and I led her back towards that.

'It doesn't matter too much about the cottage,' I said on the way. 'I reckon I've taken some pretty good stuff already.'

'What?' she said. And then, 'Yes I suppose so. But Shakespeare isn't *here*, is he?'

I stared. 'Well, of *course* he isn't,' I said. 'He's dead. If he was still around, he'd be about four hundred and twenty years old.'

She didn't say anything. There was that funny look in her eyes again. And I had a sudden conviction that she didn't think my remark was all that witty. It occurred to me that perhaps from her point of view the morning had not been a success.

We got to the eating place, and I told her firmly that I was paying. If it had just been me I'd have brought sandwiches but I do have a certain amount of *savoir-faire*, and I reckon you can't ask a girl out for the day and feed her on sandwiches. So I'd come prepared for this.

Well, I wasn't prepared enough. I thought I had enough money to eat in that kind of place. But I'd rather lost touch with what it costs to eat out anywhere. And I might have guessed from the casual way she'd suggested spending ninety-five pence on a guide-book that it wouldn't occur to her to look too closely at the prices. She chose chicken and french fries, and then she fancied a chunk of lemon meringue pie. And coffee. I did a bit of rapid arithmetic and realized that all I could afford for myself was a small-size hamburger on a bun.

She didn't notice at first. She was rather thoughtful, not saying much. I wasn't saying much either. I was trying to work out how I could get through the rest of the term without borrowing again from Auntie, which I'd done too often already.

Then her eye fell on my plate and she said, 'Sam! Is that all you're having?'

'Yes,' I said. 'It's all I want.'

'But I thought you were hungry.'

'I'd forgotten,' I said, 'that I had a big breakfast before I set out.'

'Oh, *Sam*! Are you economizing? Here, you must let me pay for my own.'

I wouldn't take her money, of course. She seemed a bit upset about it at first. But in a funny kind of way it seemed to change the pattern of the day. We shared the food we had between us, which is always friendly. Afterwards we went down to the river and the canal basin and watched the boats and wandered around and chatted, and I told her about the Poly and Larry Lomas and my uncle and auntie, and she told me about her school and her parents and her gran and gramp. And we both had a bit of a laugh over her pal Susan. I said I would make an enormous blow-up of that picture of Susan against the railings, and she said that Susan would love it and I'd be her hero, and I said I could live without being Susan's hero. And so on. In fact we laughed quite a lot.

I only took a couple of pictures by the river, because it was the buildings I'd really come to photograph, and I'd done enough of them and used up most of my film. But there was a funny moment when a log came floating slowly down the river with a duck sitting on it looking quite comfortable and at home. Jenny grabbed the camera and took a quickie of it. I told her she'd be lucky if she'd got the focus and exposure right, but she wasn't bothered. 'Oh, it doesn't matter,' she said. 'If it doesn't come out, it's too bad. But the duck looked so *complacent*, didn't it? As if it had got the river trained, and the river was taking it just where it wanted to go.'

'I doubt whether ducks work it out that way,' I said. And then she made the kind of remark that I got to know later as a Jennyism.

'Life's like that, isn't it?' she said. 'Like a river, and we're on our little logs, being carried along wherever it takes us.'

She's always going on about Life. With a capital L.

'Come off it!' I said. 'If it wasn't taking *me* where I wanted to go, I'd jump off and swim.' And we both laughed some more.

When I saw her off at the coach station, she said, 'Sam, my father would like to meet you. Especially if you're going to go on using the Hasselblad. He wants to be sure he can trust you with it.' (This last bit seemed to amuse her, but I could see her dad's point.) 'So why don't you come and see us at Kingston?'

I wasn't sure I liked the idea. My folk don't mix with architects and such. My dad is a fitter at an engineering works, and he might be made redundant any time. I backed off a bit.

'I may not *need* to go on borrowing the Hasselblad,' I said. 'I'm still hoping to get the other one back. Anyway, today's pictures may fill the bill.'

I'd have sworn she looked quite hurt.

'I'll send you some prints of what I've taken,' I said. And, remembering her own attempts, I added, 'And of your clouds and duck, if they come out!'

Her expression still wasn't too happy. And suddenly I thought, hell, I don't want to leave her looking like that. I heard myself saying, 'Of course, I could *bring* the prints to you. It'd save the trouble of mailing.'

'Would it?' she said. 'Thank you, Sam Horsfall. That's a *real* compliment!'

I realized I could have put it more tactfully. Still, she was smiling now. She didn't look hurt any longer.

'And it'd be good to see you again,' I added. 'I'll ring you and we'll fix it up.'

It had been a strange day and she was a strange girl. I hadn't thought I'd want to arrange another meeting. I was quite surprised to find I did.

7

Jenny

Everyone in the class knew I was going to Stratford with Sam Horsfall. It was Susan who found out, earlier in the week. She suggested a Saturday morning's window-shopping, and when I made an excuse she jumped uncannily to the right conclusion. She had the details out of me in no time, and had spread them around to all and sundry in not much more. The class were interested, because they'd all seen the pictures and heard Susan's lurid accounts of Sam, and anyway it seemed to be something of a nine days' wonder that dreamy Jenny Midhurst was going anywhere with a boy of any kind.

So by the time that Saturday came round, and I'd got up early but not quite early enough, and breakfasted in one minute flat on a bowl of cornflakes, and caught a train and changed to a coach and was on my way to Stratford, I was feeling a bit weary of the expedition already. And when I arrived at Stratford he wasn't there, and I had to sit on a bench at the coach station and wait.

I pondered the whole affair once more while I was waiting. Today, I said to myself, I would decide whether I liked Sam Horsfall enough to see him any more, and if I didn't I wasn't going to make any more arrangements or be moved by any more heart-rending appeals. If I did feel willing to see him again — and if of course he wanted to see me, which wasn't at all certain — then he could do the travelling next time. I would take up my father's suggestion and invite him to our house.

What, I wondered, would my father think of Sam?

My mother was fairly predictable. She'd be nice to him
— very nice — but she'd make it clear afterwards that she
didn't think he was quite our type. Dad was totally
unpredictable. He might take to Sam and he might
not . . . I was speculating on these matters when I suddenly realized that Sam was standing in front of me. I
hadn't noticed him approaching. But there he was, neat
and relatively kempt, wearing a tidy jacket and trousers
with a crease pressed in and a cheerful grin on his face.

'Hello,' he said. 'Shall I carry the camera?' He eyed it
with admiring interest, which was more than he'd ever
done for *me*. It puts me in my place, I thought. She-who-
brings-me-the-Hasselblad, that's what I am.

He gave me a hard time that morning. He marched me
round the streets of Stratford, with frequent pauses while
he took all the obvious pictures of all the obvious things.
I had just one good moment, at Shakespeare's birthplace,
when Sam decided it was my turn. Having told me rather
more than I wanted to know about the technicalities of the
matter, he shoved the camera into my hands and told me
to have a go. And, as it happened, a marvellous cloud
came over. Silvered and raggedly curled at the edges,
with a kind of hole in the middle where a shaft of sunlight
came through, and a huge range of shades, all the way
from dazzling white to bruised indigo. It wasn't like my
pebbles: it was *alive*. Irresistible. I took two pictures of
it just in time before the light suddenly went wrong and
the silver vanished and it was any old grey cloud.

Then I saw he was looking pityingly at me, as if I'd shot
at a target and missed it by half a mile.

'The house is over *there*,' he said in the tones of someone addressing a half-wit. 'All you've got in is a bit of
chimney-stack.'

'I just liked the cloud,' I said.

'There are clouds everywhere,' he told me. 'You don't
have to come to Stratford to find a cloud. Anyway, there's
nothing special about it.' And there wasn't, by then.

I gave him a look, but it bounced straight off. Obviously it took more than a look to make any impression on Sam. We continued foot-slogging.

I let my thoughts wander away. I wondered why I got so little pleasure from visiting Stratford, and decided that it actually diminished William Shakespeare. Instead of the man who'd made me weep for Juliet or Ophelia, all that the Shakespeare industry did was to boost a celebrity, like it might have been somebody well known on the telly. A celebrity, they say, is a person who is famous for being famous. That's how you get to feel about Shakespeare, star of the Bard Show. You've lost sight of what he's famous *for*.

'He isn't really *here*, is he?' I said aloud when at last Sam seemed to have had enough and we were on our way to look for something to eat.

I might have known that wouldn't make sense to Sam. He stared, and then remarked with heavy humour that W. Shakespeare was dead, and if alive would have been over four hundred years old. That was the moment, I think, when Sam Horsfall struck bottom. I wondered how I could possibly have got involved with someone who made cracks as feeble as that. If he'd suddenly given me the camera back and said good-bye for ever, I'd hardly even have bothered to wave.

But then we got to the eating-place, and I noticed that while I was tucking heartily into chicken and chips, all he had in front of him was one skinny little hamburger.

'Sam!' I said. 'Is that all you're having?'

He blushed. He positively blushed. Then he mumbled something unconvincing about having had a big breakfast before he set out.

'Oh, Sam!' I said. 'Are you economizing? Here, let me pay for mine. Please.'

There was quite a squabble about that. I gathered that there was a Horsfall Theory of Taking Out a Girl. In general, Sam was quite willing to go Dutch, but he reckoned that when the girl in question (me) was doing him a favour, and moreover travelling a considerable distance at her own expense to do so, then the sense of fair play which according to him was characteristic of all northerners, and especially Yorkshiremen, prohibited him from accepting any contribution to the cost of her meal.

I said that a sense of fair play didn't require him to go hungry, and would he please take my money and get himself something more substantial.

He said he wouldn't.

I said it was all right, I could afford it, I had plenty left out of my allowance.

He said he didn't doubt I could afford it, being the kind of person who got an allowance rather than mere pocket-money, but as a matter of principle he wasn't going to accept.

I said he was stiff and proud. And we had a real old barney about money and class and the equality or otherwise of the sexes. It got quite heated, but the funny thing was that I felt as if we were at last getting to grips with each other. And I quite liked him for his pride, even though I did think it was silly.

I broke off the argument by pointing out that my chicken and chips were getting cold, and if we went on much longer neither of us would have anything worth eating. Then we both laughed, and as he still wouldn't give way I fed him with french fries and bits of chicken from my plate. He said he hadn't been treated like that since he was a little boy, and insisted on giving me bites of hamburger. After that he didn't jib at sharing my lemon meringue pie. When we'd finished eating we went on with the argument, which had become quite amiable.

And the day had been saved. Sam decided he'd taken enough pictures of buildings, so we went and wandered by the water, talking fifteen to the dozen about everything under the sun. He took a river scene or two, and I got another picture myself although I had to grab the camera from him to get it. It was a duck sitting on a drifting log and looking comically complacent. I thought it made a good picture. And from that I got to thinking that a duck going downstream was like us going through life, and that Sam and I on our little separate logs had happened to bump up against each other, but maybe we would merely drift apart again.

In spite of the way I'd felt a couple of hours previously, I found myself deciding that I didn't want that to happen, and that I would after all do as my father suggested and invite Sam to Kingston. So at the coach station I asked him. There was a bit of humming and hawing, which wasn't very flattering really. In the end, he talked about bringing me the prints and said he'd get in touch with me, but he didn't say when.

All right, Sam Horsfall, I thought, the ball's in your court. I have my pride, too. I'm not going to do anything more until I hear from you.

I hoped I *would* hear from him, though. I still didn't quite know why.

8

Sam

I got a ride almost at once, all the way to Barhampton, from a grey-haired head teacher on her way home from a conference. She was all right. I liked her. She told me what was wrong with present-day students and I told her what was wrong with present-day teachers. I dare say she didn't listen to me any more than I listened to her, but we both had a good time.

I was quite satisfied with my day at Stratford. I was sure I'd taken some good pictures. And I was all set up to cope with Auntie. Maybe when I stand in the dock on the Day of Judgement my Defending Angel will point out that for once I was patient and good-tempered and I didn't either stop my ears or explode with impatience at Auntie's questioning. I'd gathered a bit of information about the Jenny way of life in the course of the day, and I dutifully told Auntie as much as I could remember. It wasn't enough for her — not by any means — but at least she knew I'd tried.

In the end, of course, she wanted to know when I was going to see Jenny again.

'Well,' I said, 'she did ask me to go to her house and meet her parents.'

That had Auntie in two minds right away. On the one hand it proved — not, she said, that it needed proving — that Jenny was a *nice* girl, and I should certainly go. I could tell from the light in her eye that she was looking forward already to a report on the curtains and carpets of Jenny's home. On the other hand she wished I'd got in first with an invitation. She hoped it wouldn't be long before I brought Jenny here.

I didn't think it would be much of a thrill for Jenny or anyone else to come and experience Auntie's enormous curiosity and Uncle Frank's total lack of it. But I didn't want to hurt Auntie's feelings by saying so. I managed to get out of the conversation without either offending her or actually promising anything.

Meanwhile I had my pictures. As soon as I got the negs on Monday I could see that I'd done a good job. In fact, a chap less modest than me would say they were brilliant. Sharp, clear, contrasty — they were going to print up a treat.

I chose my time carefully for making the prints. At the Poly, we work on individual enlargers and then put the exposed prints into a slot in a big machine that develops them and spits out the results. Most of the time there are two or three people standing around the machine waiting for their own prints and getting a look at everybody else's in the meantime. I'd decided that for purposes of the competition I was going to keep my successes to myself, so as not to stimulate the opposition.

The Department is open in the evening on Mondays, Wednesdays and Fridays. It's less busy then than in the daytime. Especially on Mondays, when the girls are all at home washing their hair and the guys are recovering from the weekend, if they're lucky enough to be able to afford the kind of weekend you have to recover from. So after tea at Auntie's on Monday, I hiked back into town and got to work.

I'd judged dead right from the negs. My pictures were terrific. Even Jenny's weren't too bad. I made prints for her of the clouds and the duck, and I made extra prints of some of my own pictures to give her. I didn't intend to point out the superiority of my own work; I reckoned it would speak for itself. I would offer her a bit of encouragement, I decided, and perhaps a few suggestions as to how she could do better.

I got my sheaf of prints together and put them in an envelope in my folder. I switched everything off, being the last person in the Department that night. Then I realized I had a headache coming on. In fact I didn't feel too good at all. I went home to Auntie's on the bus instead of walking as I usually do.

By next morning the headache was ferocious and I also had a sore throat and kept feeling hot and cold by turns. There were dire things going on in my guts too. I knew I had the Plague. I don't mean the bubonic plague. The Plague was the name we were giving in the Poly to a bug that was going around. It was a kind of gastric flu with knobs on. It laid you on your back for three or four days, during which you felt that by comparison death was rather tempting. Then it went off and did it to somebody else.

I was indignant at being attacked by this bug. Where I come from, we're a tough and healthy lot. I hardly ever have anything wrong with me. I couldn't believe it at first, but when I tried to get out of bed and crumpled at the knees so that I had to crawl back in again quick, I had to admit that the Plague had got me.

Auntie looked after me marvellously, of course. She was alarmed and at the same time she was in her element. 'We've got to get you right for your birthday next week,' she said. I'd forgotten that it was going to be my birthday — my twentieth — although I shouldn't have done, because Auntie had been engaged for weeks on a top-secret knitting project, which was clearly going to be a sweater for me.

Anyway, Auntie telephoned the Poly, which was not surprised by the news, because half its students were off with the Plague already. On Friday morning she came into my room with a letter and stood by hopefully while I opened it. Inside was a get-well card. It was signed, 'Love, Elaine'.

That was a surprise. Elaine's apparent interest in me had faded fast after our little encounter at Pam's

Pantry earlier in the term. She had struck up a beautiful friendship with Phil Radley, who had a well-equipped darkroom in his parents' house right here in Barhampton. Elaine had a Mini, financed by Daddy over at Cheltenham. One with a darkroom but no Mini, one with a Mini but no darkroom — Elaine and Phil were obviously made for each other.

I handed Auntie the card. She was half bemused, half disapproving. '*Another* young lady!' she said. '*Well*!'

An hour later, bringing me a hot drink, she asked, 'Who is this Elaine, then?'

'Listen, Auntie,' I said, 'I've mentioned her before. You must have forgotten. She's just a girl in our department at the Poly. She isn't a special friend. In fact' — it was a bit mean of me to say this, but I wanted to scotch any wrong ideas — 'in fact I don't much like her.'

'She seems to like *you*,' said Auntie. 'Love, she says. Love, indeed!'

'Don't be daft,' I said. ' "Love" doesn't mean anything these days. It's just the same as "Yours sincerely".'

'Oh, is it?' she said dubiously. 'Well, *I* don't know. Times change!'

After another hour, coming in to see what I fancied for dinner, she inquired, 'Have you let Jenny know you're ill in bed?'

'No,' I said. 'Should I have done?'

I hadn't forgotten that I was going to fix up a visit to Jenny. But I'd been laid so low by the Plague that I hadn't wanted to think about going anywhere. And, to be honest, I was just a shade nervous about meeting her mum and dad. They sounded a bit alarming.

'Jenny must like you,' Auntie said, 'or she wouldn't have gone to so much trouble for you.'

After yet another hour, coming in with a meal on a tray, Auntie remarked, 'I wonder what they see in you, Sam Horsfall. I wouldn't have thought you were all that good-looking, myself.'

I could have thrown the Lucozade at her.

I was up by the weekend, though still a bit feeble. On Monday morning I insisted on going in to the Poly. The first thing I did was to retrieve my folder, which I'd left lying on a bench when I began to feel ill, and take out the packet of Stratford prints. They didn't seem to have been tampered with. Then I put my head round Larry's door to report that I was back.

'Feeling all right now, Sam?' he said, and then, 'any news?'

By that he meant, any news about the missing equipment. Until I got the Plague he'd asked me every day. Not usually in words. He would just raise a questioning eyebrow and I'd shake my head. I did so now.

Larry said, 'Sam, quite apart from that, I gather you're hard up.'

'You can say that again,' I told him.

'You'd like to earn a bit of money?'

I nodded.

'Well, the Plague may have put you in the way of it. Go round to the *Echo* office, Sam. Ask for Ken Edwards. He's the picture editor.'

For a moment I felt even weaker at the knees than the Plague had left me. I knew, as everybody did in the Department, that the picture editor of the *Echo* was a pal of Larry's. But I'd never met him. The *Echo* was a different world from ours.

'You mean . . . I've to do a job for the *Echo?*'

'Could be, Sam. I don't know. Ken asked me to send someone round who can handle a camera.'

'B-but . . . why me?'

'For heaven's sake, Sam! Why you, indeed? Because you're the first person I've seen this morning. Because everyone else is either dead or dying. Because you're a twit and I'm soft-hearted and I want to help you. Ask silly questions and you'll get silly answers. Just go and see Ken, before I change my mind and send somebody else. And take some prints along with you. Good ones.'

'I'll go and sort some out,' I said.

'What's that in your hand?' Larry asked.

It was the envelope with the Stratford prints in it. I told him so.

'What are they like?'

'First-rate,' I said. 'I'll probably put some of them in for the competition.'

'Then don't show me them, Sam. I've told you all, I'm not going to look at anybody's entries in advance. But it sounds as if they'd be all right. Take them to Ken. He'll want to see what you can do.'

The front office of the *Barhampton Echo* is in the High Street, next to Woolworth's. It's very smart: all plate-glass and mahogany and wall-to-wall carpet, and dolly-birds poised ready to help you advertise your second-hand motor-bike or three-piece suite. The side entrance is round the corner in a narrow street that's not much more than an alleyway. Inside it is a dimly lit passage that leads you to the part of the building where they actually produce the newspaper. From somewhere in the bowels of the earth you can hear, if it's the right time of day, the printing presses roaring away and making the floor vibrate.

On the next floor up there's a big room where they set the type and make up the pages. The *Echo* hasn't gone over to new technology yet, so there's still a battery of old-fashioned typesetting machines, clanking away fit to bust. And on the floor above that is another big room, all shrill with telephones and chattering with typewriters, where the reporters and sub-editors work. Around this big room there's a fringe of small scruffy offices, and after I'd asked two or three people I arrived at one of the smallest and scruffiest of them, which was that of Ken Edwards. It had three telephones, two chairs and one desk, which was buried about eighteen inches deep under piles of photographs. Ken Edwards himself stood at a kind of lectern, making marks with a pencil on the back of a print that was lit up for him from underneath.

I was more than somewhat interested in Ken Edwards. If I won the competition and got a trial on the paper, this man would be my boss. He was a bit older than Larry: mid-thirties at a guess, big and thickening at the midriff. He had a round, reddish face that would have been fairly ordinary if he hadn't surrounded it with a huge curly ginger beard. His eyes were bright and blue, smallish and shrewd. He looked amiable enough.

'I'm Sam Horsfall,' I said. 'Larry Lomas sent me.'

'Hello, Sam,' he said. 'Won't keep you a minute. Sit down.'

I couldn't sit down, because the chairs, like the desk, were covered with photographs. Ken noticed the difficulty, came across, and shifted them to join the rest on the desk. He returned to the lighting device, pencilled an outline on the back of the print, dropped it into a tray and pressed a button.

'Just had to mark a cut-out,' Ken said. He sat down in the other chair, leaned back and surveyed me. A messenger came in, took the print from the tray, and left about thirty others in its place.

'A quiet day so far,' Ken Edwards remarked. His eye fell, as Larry's had done, on the envelope in my hand.

'Are those your work, Sam?' he asked; and when I nodded, 'let's have a look at them.' He cleared a space on his desk. A bunch of pictures fell on the floor, and Ken left them there. I spread out my own in the space he'd cleared.

Ken Edwards said, 'Stratford.'

I nodded.

'Taken with a good camera.'

I nodded again. There was a kind of noisy silence,

with the racket from the typewriters and telephones in the big room going on as Ken pondered. Then, 'I like the cloudscapes.'

I blinked. I'd forgotten that Jenny's pictures were in the batch.

'And I like the duck,' Ken went on. 'I like that a lot. Let me have a print of that for stock, Sam. One of these days we might manage to use it, with a feature article or something.'

I blinked again. I'd always thought that picture editors were dyed-in-the wool professionals who'd want a good reproducible picture with plenty of content. Not whimsies about clouds and ducks. I wondered if Ken Edwards was really up to his job. Still, it wasn't for me to judge. He was in charge, and if I went to the *Echo* he was the man I'd have to work for.

He must have misread my expression. 'Don't worry, Sam,' he said. 'We'll pay you a print fee. And if we do use it in the paper, you'll be paid for that.' Then he went on, 'Your pictures are all right, Sam, and Larry tells me you're a good lad. Well, I have an assignment for you, if you want it.'

'Oh, I want it all right,' I said.

'It's a one-off, remember. There won't be another to follow, so don't get any wrong ideas. This is an emergency. You know everyone's down with flu just now. Tom Sigsworth and Harry Adams are in bed, and both the local freelances are out of action. Young Derek Dixon is still working — touch wood — but he's rushed off his feet, and there's a job I can't cover. Not an exciting one, I'm afraid, but straightforward. It's on Wednesday. The Mayor's opening the new shopping precinct, just off the market-place.'

'And you want me to cover the opening?' I asked.

'No, Sam. That's a professional's job. Trickier than you might think. The Mayor this year is Councillor Green, and he's a tetchy old devil. Derek can manage him, though. He'll do it.'

'Then what. . . ?'

'Point is, Sam, they're only taking the wraps off the precinct the same morning. It's all concealed behind hoardings at present. KEEP OUT signs everywhere. I want a set of pictures of the precinct for the centre-page spread, and I want them in time for the early edition. Derek will do the news picture in the afternoon, but I can't spare him in the morning; there's too many other jobs to do. Now, you get the idea, Sam? You go along there bright and early on Wednesday and take lots of pictures from all angles. Bring them in here, develop and print them — fast — and then you've finished. Leave the choosing to me. You'll be paid at freelance rates, and with a bit of luck you'll do quite well out of it.'

'Th-thank you,' I said. I was rather overwhelmed.

'You'll be using the camera you had at Stratford, I suppose,' Ken Edwards said conversationally. 'What is it, Sam?'

'A Hasselblad.'

'Lucky sod,' said Ken. 'I wish *I* could afford one of those.'

I couldn't bring myself to tell him I didn't actually have the camera at my disposal. And just then, two of his three telephones started ringing simultaneously, an intercom buzzed, and somebody came in shouting that there'd been a rail crash in South Wales.

'You see what it's like, lad,' said Ken Edwards. 'No rest for the wicked.' He reached out, unhurriedly, for one of the telephones. 'Off you go, Sam. See you on Wednesday.'

It was a weird kind of day. I was still feeling a bit woozy after the Plague. I was excited by the thought of an assignment for the *Echo*, earning a bit of money and possibly helping myself along the way to a job. But I was apprehensive about it, too. I wondered whether I had the nerve to ask Jenny to Barhampton so soon after

72

the Stratford trip, or whether I should do the job as best I could with my own old camera. I knew it was no good trying to borrow anything more from the Poly.

When I got back to Auntie's at teatime, Uncle Frank was just home from work. I told them both at once about the *Echo* assignment. They weren't as impressed as I'd expected. They didn't read the *Echo*, which they considered inferior to the *Yorkshire Evening Post*. Uncle Frank observed darkly that you couldn't believe everything you read in the papers, especially in this part of the world. I couldn't quite see what that had to do with it. As for Auntie Edith, she seemed actually upset by the news.

'On your birthday, too!' she said.

I stared. 'What's wrong with that?' I asked. 'You don't expect me to stay at home all day, Auntie, do you?'

'No but . . .' She hesitated. Then, 'I have a surprise for you.' Another pause, and she went on, 'Maybe I'd better tell you now.'

'Go on,' I said. 'I'm all agog.' I thought the surprise would be the sweater she'd been knitting. It would be just like her to make a great production out of a sweater. And it wasn't exactly the thrill of a lifetime. I'd have preferred it in some colour other than mauve.

But it wasn't the sweater.

'I'm making you a birthday tea,' Auntie announced. From her tone of voice, she might have been talking to a seven-year-old. 'And I've asked somebody to come. A special birthday guest.'

'Auntie! Who?'

'Guess.'

I groaned. 'Not Uncle Jack?'

'No!' she said. 'No! Guess again!'

'I haven't the least idea.'

'It's a young lady,' she said. '*Now* can you guess?'

'Oh, my God! You don't mean you've invited . . .'

'Yes! Jenny! I telephoned her last night!'

73

'Listen!' I said. 'You can't *do* things like that! Inviting somebody for *my* birthday! It isn't up to you!'

Obviously that hadn't occurred to Auntie.

'I thought it would be nice for you both,' she said plaintively. 'After all, you did go all the way to Stratford to meet each other.'

'But don't you realize,' I said, 'that you've no right to organize people's lives for them? Jenny mightn't want to come. And what if I'd made other plans? If it wasn't for being ill, I expect I *would* have done. I'd probably have been going out for a drink or two with Larry and the boys.'

'And that Elaine, I dare say!' said Auntie. She sniffed disapprovingly. 'Anyway, Jenny said she'd come.'

I shook my head in despair. There was nothing to be done about Auntie. She simply didn't understand what constituted reasonable behaviour. Now her lip was quivering. She was hurt by my reaction to her efforts. In another minute she'd be lamenting that everything she ever did was wrong and she might just as well not be here at all.

And then of course the thought struck me. Auntie might unwittingly have saved the day. If Jenny came, I could presumably have the Hasselblad after all. I relented.

'Auntie Edith,' I said, 'you're impossible. But I suppose I have to forgive you!' And I hugged her.

After supper I went to the telephone. Jenny's mother answered. I hadn't spoken to her before. She sounded rather cool and southern, but she admitted that Jenny was around and put her on the line.

'Oh, Sam!' Jenny said. 'I'm glad you've rung. I didn't know what to say to your aunt. But it's half-term, and I *can* come. Do you really want me to?'

I thought of the *Echo* and of the shopping precinct. I didn't want to mislead Jenny as to my motives. But I did want her to come, no doubt about that.

'Of course I do!' I said.

'At least, I don't have to bring the Hasselblad this time!' said Jenny.

'Well. . . ,' I said. 'Actually it might be quite a good idea if you did. And arrived as early as possible.'

9

Jenny

Strange are the silences of Sam.

I don't know quite how that phrase came into my mind, but I kept saying it to myself as the days went by after our trip to Stratford. I expected to hear his voice on the telephone, reporting on the prints he'd made and presumably suggesting a date for delivering them; but it didn't happen.

Oddly, it never occurred to me that Sam might be ill, while it occurred to me continually that, having got his pictures, he might simply not be bothering any more. And that hurt. And yet I still wasn't all *that* interested in Sam. Not as such. Perhaps, I said to myself, it's only as a stage in life that this episode seems to matter. When I'm in my twenties and have lots of men friends, I shall look back and remember, with a smile and an effort, that a certain Sam — what was his name, I shall ask myself? Horsley? Horton? No, Horsfall — was the first young man I ever went anywhere with, even if it was only to take photographs . . .

It was half-term, and cold grey weather, and I was in disgrace with Susan because Sam still had the negative of the famous railings picture and she hadn't yet got her prints. Susan was now going around with Tanya Frith. I didn't think that would last long, because Tanya was only going around with Susan in the absence of her own best friend Ann Smedley, and when Ann came back Tanya would return to Ann and Susan would return to me. In the meantime, my life consisted of home and school, and

I had to admit it was a bit dull. And now there was a whole week's holiday stretching bleakly ahead.

The phone call came at the beginning of that week. A warm, homely, northern, middle-aged, female voice. A bit hesitant at first. Announcing itself as Sam Horsfall's Aunt Edith, and going on to explain that Sam had had flu. Myself expressing surprise and concern. The voice, gathering pace and confidence, giving a full account of the progress of the flu and of Sam's recovery.

Sam had told me quite a lot about Auntie Edith, and I'd got the impression that she was a tiresome old windbag. But I liked this voice. Motherly I'd have called it if I hadn't known that Auntie Edith didn't have any children of her own. She didn't sound at all like my own mother, who is kind and well-meaning but conventional and rather reserved, and who certainly doesn't pour out her heart to strangers. As Auntie Edith was pouring hers out to me. Details now of Sam's childhood tastes and preferences, and of the meals she'd given him when he was ill in bed but starting to feel hungry again. It all washed warmly over me.

And then, the point of the call. It was Sam's birthday on Wednesday, and would I go to Barhampton for the day as a nice surprise for him?

That caught me unprepared. I couldn't find anything to say at first. But Auntie Edith's voice filled the silence comfortably. She was telling me now what an excellent lad Sam was, careful and conscientious and never one for the girls, but she knew he liked *me* . . .

In that case, I thought, why doesn't he get in touch? But of course, he'd been down with flu. And if it was a birthday surprise for him, he couldn't do the inviting himself, could he? On the other hand, why should I keep dashing around the country? And could I be sure Sam really wanted me to go? And . . . and . . . and . . .

While I was thinking all this, Auntie Edith's voice went on. Hoping I would go for the day, and telling me about trains from London, and hinting at help with the fare if it was too expensive. And somehow, as with Sam himself before the Stratford trip, I found myself assenting. And found myself wondering, after a final flow of thanks and good wishes and looking-forward-to-meeting-me, how I could possibly have been so foolish.

It was a relief when Sam himself rang the next day and said his auntie had told him and he certainly wanted me to come.

'I don't have to bring the Hasselblad this time, do I?' I asked. I said it as a kind of joke, and it was a shock when he said it might be a good idea if I did. So he's *still* after the wretched camera, I thought. I didn't think it any less when he said mysteriously that he had an important assignment to carry out. For two pins I'd have wriggled out of the whole thing. But I didn't. I just agreed to go up to Barhampton on an early train and to take the Hasselblad once more. Strange are the compliances of Jenny.

My mother, pointedly, said nothing at all when I told her. Not 'How nice, dear,' or even 'Do you really have to?' Dad, however, came about as close as he knows how to get to the heavy father.

'That's three away matches in a row,' he said. 'Next time he comes here. Okay?'

'Okay,' I said.

Sam was anxious and edgy when he met me at the station.

'Your train was ten minutes late,' he said accusingly.

'I apologize on behalf of British Rail. I'm sorry there was nothing I could do about it.'

'Oh, it wasn't your fault,' he admitted, though I had the impression that deep down he was convinced that if I'd been better organized the train would have got there sooner. 'We'll have to hurry, though. I'm pushed for time.'

'All right,' I said. 'But, Sam, happy birthday! It's your twentieth, isn't it?'

'Yes.'

'Sweet and twenty,' I said on impulse.

'What?' He was outraged. 'Me? Sweet?'

'I was only quoting. That man from Stratford. "Then come kiss me, sweet and twenty." '

I was teasing, of course, but Sam reddened. Then, hurrying me out of the station, he told me somewhat breathlessly that he had this job of photographing a new shopping precinct for the local evening paper.

'We'll have to step it out,' he said. 'It's nearly ten o'clock, and I've to get to the precinct, take my pictures, and have them developed by eleven.'

'How far away is it?'

'A good half-mile.'

'We could get a taxi,' I said. There was a line of them at the cab-rank. But Sam looked alarmed at the prospect of taking a taxi. I remembered his financial embarrassment at Stratford and wished I hadn't made the suggestion. We walked. Fast.

When we got to the precinct, a couple of great big lorries were just driving away, loaded with what looked like hoardings, and a little knot of men were sweeping up debris. So we wouldn't actually have done any better if we'd arrived earlier. It was another five minutes before the precinct showed a clean and shining face to the world. A rather ordinary face, I thought. I've seen a few shopping precincts in my time. My father designs them, but this wasn't one of his. It was a paved area with trees in tubs and seats and a little pond, and there were two tiers of shops round it in a horseshoe shape, with the upper ring of shops reached by a gallery. There were a few sightseers around but hardly any shoppers. It looked as if most of the shops were still unlet.

It was a grey day; we'd had a lot of them lately. Sam moved briskly around, taking picture after picture from angle after angle. Once or twice he asked people, rather nervously, to look in a shop window or admire a tree. I didn't feel tempted to grab the camera. There was only one shot of the precinct that looked interesting to me, and that was where the ramp from the upper gallery came down in a nice gentle curve to the paved area. Just at that one point there was a bit of real elegance.

I told Sam he should photograph that, and he said he'd have done so anyway. As we were looking, a little ancient scruffy man came tottering down the ramp. Heaven knows what he'd been doing up aloft, but down he hobbled in broken boots, bent almost double and looking as if he'd fall on his face any moment.

'I'll just let him get out of the way,' Sam said.

'No, don't do that. It makes a nice contrast doesn't it? All this modern splendour, and the human element is just a little funny old man like him.'

Sam gave me what I'd come to recognize as his pitying look, but he hadn't time to discuss the matter. He took the picture, and went on to take others at other places. And then he said, 'Right. I'm off to the *Echo* office. Mind if I take the camera and unload it there?'

'Shall I come too?' I asked.

But he wasn't receptive to that idea. He seemed to think this wasn't the occasion for taking a girl along. Well, perhaps it wasn't, but he clearly hadn't given any thought to the question of what he was going to do with me. He pointed me towards a bus stop, told me which number bus to take, where to get off it, and how to find his aunt's house. And then he disappeared, literally at a run. I felt like a dumped and unwanted parcel. Especially as it was twenty minutes before a bus came, and then I went past the stop and had to walk half a mile back. It was beginning to rain, too. Quite a celebration, I thought, as I plodded through the rain in a dreary town looking for the house of a person I'd never met.

It was a suburb of Barhampton, a maze of avenues and crescents, all curling around each other like an intricate pattern on wallpaper. I should think you could live there for years and still get lost if you strayed a quarter of a mile from your home. The houses were semi-detached, with neat front lawns and garages. Everything was end-lessly repeated. It wasn't really a place at all, I thought. It could have been anywhere.

In spite of Sam's instructions, I had trouble in finding his aunt's house. It was the needle-in-a-haystack syndrome. But I got there in the end; and she was expecting me. The door burst open almost as I touched it, and I was told to come in and take off my coat and sit down by the fire and have a cup of tea.

Sam's Aunt Edith was a solid woman, thickset rather than fat. Not pretty, but good-looking in a serviceable kind of way. Greying hair, high colour in cheeks, expression lively and benevolent. Lots of energy. I liked her. From the way she said, 'You look *just* as I expected, dear,' I took it she liked me.

With the tea came conversation. I could tell at once that for Auntie Edith talk was action, and she had unlimited amounts of it, all dammed up and urgent to get out. From time to time she interrogated me, but mostly she informed me. In the next hour I learned more about Sam than he would ever want me to know. It was obvious that he was the apple of his aunt's eye. Out it came: all the amazing things he'd done and said since he first began to walk and talk. His life-story was illustrated by a proudly shown album containing pictures of Sam at every stage of his development from naked infant on hearthrug to hefty young man overtopping his mother and aunt. He'd always been clever, his aunt said; moreover, he was thoughtful and considerate . . .

It occurred to me that she was giving Sam a better testimonial than he'd given her. I liked her still more.

Apart from Sam, Aunt Edith's main topic of conversation was life in the good old days in industrial York-shire, from which she had so long been exiled. The friendly streets where you knew everybody, the relatives all within reach, the neighbours dropping in, the shops on every corner, the washing hung across the streets on

Monday mornings. Her eyes were full of yearning for a lost way of life. Nobody coming from the South could really understand, she said.

Time passed, and Sam himself didn't appear. Aunt Edith became a little concerned. It wasn't like Sam, she said, to be late home. She hoped this newspaper business hadn't led to some kind of trouble. She wasn't sure she really liked such an involvement. Several times we peered out of the front window to see if there was any sign of him. And on the last of these occasions, it was to see Sam paying off a taxi. He came running up the garden path, waving a copy of the *Echo*. Aunt Edith went to the door, and I heard her welcoming him roguishly: 'A *taxi*, eh, Sam Horsfall? You *must* have been in a hurry to get back to your young lady!'

'It's *expenses*!' I heard Sam tell her. 'Ken said I could take one and claim for it!' And then he burst into the room, shot a quick "Hello, Jenny!" at me, and spread out the *Echo* on the table. There they were: five pictures of the precinct, filling the top half of both the centre pages, under the headline PARADISE FOR CITY SHOPPERS.

'You wouldn't think there'd have been *time*, would you?' said Aunt Edith.

'Oh, they *move* at the *Echo*,' said Sam knowledgeably. He gave an account of the selection of negatives, the high-speed developing and printing and blockmaking, and the unerring rapidity with which Ken Edwards had drawn his page layout. Sam had been allowed into the process department to see the blocks made and into the composing room to see the page assembled. He gave us blow-by-blow accounts of these mysteries.

'And you see that?' he finished proudly. Under the bottom right-hand picture was the credit line. It was tiny but it was there: 'Pictures by Sam Horsfall'.

The biggest of the five pictures was the one that showed the foot of the ramp that came down from the gallery to the paved area. It did indeed look elegant: the best feature of the precinct. I was glad they'd given the place of honour to that one. But there was something missing. After a few seconds it dawned on me.

'What happened to the little old man?' I asked.

'Oh,' said Sam, 'they painted him out.'

'They *what*?'

'Painted him out. That was Bill Mercer's job. He does the retouching.'

'It was pretty drastic retouching, wasn't it?' I said.

'Well, you see, Ken thought he spoiled the picture. The feature's on the shopping precinct, not on local down-and-outs. He told Bill to get rid of him. I watched. He has an artist's brush and little pots of paint. It didn't take a minute. The old geezer just kind-of vanished from the print, like . . . like . . .'

'Like the Cheshire Cat in *Alice*?' I suggested.

'I suppose so,' said Sam vaguely.

I was uneasy. 'It doesn't feel quite right, somehow. *Eliminating* an old man.'

'Don't be daft, Jenny. It doesn't do him any harm, does it? It's only to improve the picture.'

'Well, yes . . .' I had to admit to myself that it hadn't done the old man any harm. And yet it still bothered me.

Then there was a loud rat-tat on the front door. Sam went to it. I heard the voice of the taxi-driver: 'This is yours, son, isn't it?' And the voice of Sam, stammering out profuse thanks. He came back into the room, red-faced and embarrassed.

'I left the Hasselblad in the taxi,' he said.

Aunt Edith stared at him with a mixture of horror and relief, as if a hole had opened in the floor but fortunately nobody had fallen into it. I broke into nervous laughter. I didn't actually think it was funny, but I couldn't help myself.

Sam said, recovering his self-possession, 'Now if the chap in the car at Brighton had been as smart as *this* fellow, I wouldn't have lost the other one.'

That left me speechless.

* * *

I'd half expected that midday dinner at Aunt Edith's would consist of tripe or cow-heels or black pudding or some other daunting northern delicacy. Actually it was toad-in-the-hole and it was good, though decidedly solid. And during the meal Sam said he'd like to go back to the precinct and watch the official opening by the Mayor. 'I want to see how a staff photographer handles it,' he said.

'That's not very exciting for Jenny,' Aunt Edith objected.

'Oh, Jenny's interested,' said Sam, without consulting me. I didn't mind too much going with him. I supposed that the resources of Barhampton on a grey November day were pretty limited anyway. We went back into the city on the bus, since obviously the largesse of the *Echo* didn't extend to any more taxis; and we were just in nice time for the ceremony.

The open end of the precinct had been closed off with a length of ribbon, backed up by three or four policemen, and a plaque in a wall was covered by a blue curtain. A couple of bored-looking officials stood by, and a knot of maybe a dozen bystanders had gathered round. We joined them. Minutes passed: there was some stamping of feet in the cold and looking at watches; most of the bystanders drifted away but were replaced by others. At last a little procession of cars drew up, headed by the mayoral Rolls-Royce, and out stepped the Mayor, impressive in his chain of office. Other dignitaries arranged themselves around the scene. A tall, spectacularly handsome young man with a lock of dark hair falling into his eyes came bustling up and started rearranging them.

'That's Derek Dixon from the *Echo*,' Sam told me. 'I met him this morning. See his camera? It's a Rollei. Lovely job.'

Derek Dixon got the party sorted out to his satisfaction.

'Now, what about a handshake?' he said.

The Mayor took and held the hand of a gentleman who

appeared to represent the company that had built the precinct. Derek Dixon fiddled with the Rollei.

'Come on, Derek!' said the Mayor. 'Folk'll think him and me fancy each other!'

'Won't be a sec, Mayor,' said Derek. 'Just a shade this way, will you?' He took three shots of the handshake from different angles; click, click, click.

More people were gathering round; there were now about twenty spectators. The handshake was discontinued. The gentleman from the company made an extremely brief speech saying what a privilege it had been to build the precinct in Barhampton. The Mayor made an even briefer speech saying Barhampton was glad to have it. He then declared the precinct open and cut the ribbon. Derek photographed him. Click. The party reformed beside the plaque and the Mayor lifted a hand to draw the curtain. Click. The plaque was triumphantly revealed.

'Just stand aside from it, Mayor, will you?' said Derek. 'Let's get it all in. I want the lettering to be readable.'

'You'd need a double-column for that,' said the Mayor, who seemed to have experience of these matters. 'They won't give you a double-column. Not in mid-week, they won't.'

'No harm in hoping,' said Derek. Click, click. 'Now what about a full-face? Turn this way, Mayor.' Click. 'Thank you.'

It was over. The official party retreated to its cars and Derek Dixon to his. Somebody removed the curtain and the fluttering ends of the ribbon the Mayor had cut. The bystanders melted away. The plaque remained to inform posterity that His Worship the Mayor had indeed opened the precinct on this day.

'They only really *do* it for the photograph,' Sam told me.

'You're quite an expert on newspapers and civic affairs, aren't you?' I said drily. For once Sam Horsfall knew that I was teasing.

'Since this morning,' he said, and grinned.

* * *

On the next trip back to Aunt Edith's, for the birthday tea, we didn't even take the bus.

'I like walking, myself,' said Sam. I remembered once more the state of his finances. 'So do I,' I said.

We arrived to find that Uncle Frank was home from work. He greeted me with the words 'How do?' and, after a long, long silence, during which he surveyed me very deliberately from top to toe and back again without any change of expression, 'You'll have to take us as you find us.' Then he sat down and reached for the switch of the television set. Aunt Edith put her hand in the way.

'Now then, Frank Turnbull. You are not watching the telly just yet,' said Aunt Edith. 'Not when we have a young lady guest.'

'I don't mind,' I said. But Uncle Frank, still expressionless, was drawing his hand back obediently. He sat upright in his chair and looked at me thoughtfully for a little longer.

'Not a very nice day,' he said eventually.

'No,' I agreed.

There the conversation rested until Sam, who'd disappeared briefly from the room, came back looking self-conscious and wearing the mauve sweater his aunt had knitted him for his birthday. It came down almost to his knees. I duly admired it, and remembered that I'd brought him a small birthday present myself. The local camera shop had recommended it when I told them how much I could afford. It was a pistol grip, designed to help you hold a camera steady when you'd got a zoom lens on it.

Sam expressed thanks and interest. 'All I want now is the zoom lens,' he said, and grinned. Aunt Edith, taking her cue from the mention of cameras, thrust the early edition of the *Echo* into Uncle Frank's hands and drew his attention to the centre spread. Uncle Frank studied it gravely in his usual unhurried way.

'You should have seen Sam taking the pictures,' I said. 'He looked a real professional.'

For about a minute and a half I thought Uncle Frank was going to make a comment. At one point he got as far as opening his mouth, but it closed again without anything coming out. The silence continued. Aunt Edith had been bustling to and from the kitchen, and now announced the beginning of the birthday tea. There was salmon, cold ham, cold tongue and cold chicken, then fruit salad and bread and butter and jam. Finally, Aunt Edith brought in the cake, dressed overall with its twenty candles, and launched into 'Happy birthday to you!' I joined in, and so, after a while, in dirge-like tones, did Uncle Frank. 'Happy birthday, dear Sa-am, happy birthday to you!' we concluded.

Sam leaned forward, took a deep breath, and played it like a firehose on the twenty candles, extinguishing them all. We applauded. Aunt Edith, at the other side of Sam from me, planted an emphatic kiss on his cheek. Then she looked at me expectantly.

I didn't know whether this was some northern custom or whether it was Aunt Edith's own idea, but I could tell what was expected of me. I leaned towards Sam and pecked his cheek, as briefly and lightly as possible.

'There, aren't you a lucky boy!' said Aunt Edith.

Sam turned agonized eyes to me. His face was crimson. 'Sorry about all this!' he said.

Nobody had been watching Uncle Frank in the last minute or two. Suddenly the room was full of sound and a picture came up on the TV screen. He'd slipped quietly from the table to his armchair and switched the set on.

'Frank Turnbull!' cried Aunt Edith, exasperated. 'You are the *limit*!'

But Uncle Frank had done all the socializing he was going to do. Aunt Edith might as well have talked to a brick wall. He was giving his undivided attention to the set.

'Jenny love, I do apologize!' said Aunt Edith. *Men!* You can't do anything with them!'

'I'm having a lovely time,' I said. 'May I have a piece of birthday cake?'

I got the piece of birthday cake, but I didn't get to help with the washing-up. Aunt Edith refused all assistance.

'You're a visitor,' she said. 'Visitors don't wash up in *this* house. Now, Sam, what are you going to do to entertain Jenny this evening?'

'I have to catch a train at half-past eight,' I said.

'That's a long time ahead. It's only quarter to six. Well, Sam? There's a nice fire in the front room, if you and Jenny want to go in there.'

I felt embarrassed. I had a pretty good idea what the nice fire in the front room implied. Chaste embraces on the sofa, with a modest degree of privacy. I wasn't in need of the embraces or the privacy.

However, there didn't seem to be much danger. Sam groaned. 'We're not a courting couple,' he said. 'Jenny's just a *friend*, don't you understand?'

'Well, she's a very *nice* friend!' said Aunt Edith.

'Maybe we could go and see a film?' I suggested. And that saved the occasion. Sam picked up the *Echo*, and after being distracted for a minute by the need to take another look at his pictures on the centre page, turned to the cinema programmes and discovered that *Chariots of Fire* had returned to Barhampton. I didn't tell him I'd already seen it, twice.

There would just be time to see the film through and catch that train. So I left the house, complete with coat and Hasselblad, and said my farewells to Aunt Edith, who kissed me and urged me to come again as soon as possible. Uncle Frank looked up long enough to mutter ''Night!', then returned to his viewing.

'Frank's shy,' explained Aunt Edith in a whisper as we left. 'He doesn't know what to say to young ladies.'

Sam apologised for his relatives all the way to the cinema. I got impatient with him in the end. 'You're hard on them,

Sam!' I said. 'I like them a lot.' He was silent for a while after that.

Before going into the cinema, we bought two copies of the *Echo*'s last edition from a city newsvendor. One of Sam's pictures had been dropped, but the rest were still there. Derek Dixon's picture of the mayoral ceremony was at the foot of the front page. They'd used the hand-shake one, and the Mayor had been right; they'd only given it a single column. It was cropped at the sides, so that neither party to the handshake had the back of his head in the picture; but there were the two faces, smiling at each other. The mayoral chain was visible, and so were the two clasped hands.

'*I* could have taken that,' said Sam. 'Nothing to it.'

Sitting in the cinema, I let my mind wander, because although it was a marvellous film I knew it pretty well by now. I wondered whether Sam would *really* like to be a newspaper photographer. Maybe there were exciting jobs, but there were probably an awful lot of dull ordinary ones like this. And would Sam be good at organizing people into pictures and exchanging pleasantries with mayors? Did Sam in fact have much knowledge of himself? Did he muse upon things, the way I was always doing?

Now, now, Jenny, I said to myself, Sam's older and he must know what he's doing, and anyway am I any the wiser for all this musing, and don't plenty of people get through life quite happily without it?

He didn't try to hold my hand, but the one time our hands touched by accident we let them stay touched for a while.

Afterwards, at the station, Sam was more relaxed than he'd previously been. 'A red letter day, isn't it?' he said. 'I got my pictures into the *Echo*.'

'And on your birthday, too,' I said.

'Oh, yes. I'd forgotten.'

'And your friend came up from Kingston,' I said, meaning myself.

'Yes,' he said. 'Which reminds me, I didn't give you the Stratford prints after all.'

I'd forgotten about them myself.

'Never mind,' I said. 'You can still bring them to Kingston as you said you would.'

'Yes, I suppose so . . . By the way, Ken Edwards kept your picture of the duck on the log. He thought the *Echo* might use it some time.'

'Oh, good!' I said, pleased.

Sam didn't notice my response. 'Funny, isn't it?' he went on. 'Who'd have thought anyone would want *that*?'

'*Thank* you, Sam Horsfall,' I said. 'You're a great one for tact!'

Sam looked at me, almost for the first time, as if he was actually seeing me as a person. 'Sorry!' he said. He studied my face. Then, 'You're all right, Jenny,' he said. 'I like you.' And he kissed me.

Not a passionate kiss. Not on the lips, even. Not much more than the peck I'd given him at the tea-table. Not the kind of thing to impress the girls at school who told lurid tales of their real or alleged sexual experiences. But it was a kiss, and it seemed to me that Sam Horsfall didn't bestow his kisses lightly. I could still feel it on my cheek as the train drew out of Barhampton Station.

10

Sam

There's no doubt about it, that job for the *Echo* made a sensation in the Department. By the time I got in next morning, all the photography students who weren't down with the Plague had seen my pictures and taken note of the credit line. They all congratulated me, and if any of them thought I was a lucky devil, they didn't say so in my hearing. If they had, I'd have admitted it.

During the afternoon a note came down to Larry from the Deputy Director, no less. 'I have been shown the pictures on the centre page of yesterday's *Echo*,' it began (implying that the D.D. wouldn't have dreamed of opening such a rag himself). 'I understand that Sam Horsfall, who contributed them, is a student in your Department.' (Understand? He knew damn well I was.) 'Please congratulate him on my behalf.' (In other words, 'I am too important to congratulate him myself.') 'A very good job.' (Who's he to judge?)

I said nothing when Larry showed it to me, but I gave him a sideways look. Larry laughed. 'All right,' he said. 'I know. It's pompous and condescending. But it won't do the Department any harm.' I could tell he was quite pleased, really.

Several people, like me, had recovered from the Plague by now, but others had gone down with it in turn. Among them was Elaine Anders. It crossed my mind to send her a get-well card, seeing she'd sent me one the previous week, but somehow I didn't get round to it. Anyway, I didn't expect to be paid by the *Echo* before the end of the month, and until then the cost of a card and a stamp was quite a consideration.

On Friday, Elaine's pal Pat Allison came to me and said, 'Why don't you go and see Elaine?'

I said, 'Who? Me?'

Pat said, 'She'd like you to.'

I said, 'What about Phil Radley?'

Pat said, 'Didn't you know? That's all off.'

I said, 'Why?'

Pat said, 'He didn't come up to scratch.'

I said, '*He* didn't, or his darkroom didn't?'

Pat gave me a look but didn't say anything. I said, 'Anyway, why me?'

Pat Allison has a sharp tongue. She said rather tartly, 'No accounting for tastes.'

I said something very rude, which I won't repeat.

I went to see Elaine that evening, all the same. She shared a flat with Pat and another girl called Diane. It was quite a smart, well-furnished flat, not far from the city centre, and must have cost a fair bit in rent, but I suppose Daddy could afford it.

The other girl let me in and showed me which was Elaine's room. She was in bed when I arrived. She was sitting up, wearing a pink fluffy bedjacket and a nightie under it. All very pretty and feminine, not Barhampton Poly style at all. Of course, I am not susceptible to this kind of thing. Where I come from, we aren't taken in by the trimmings. But I couldn't help noticing.

She didn't look poorly at all.

'Sam!' she said. She smiled at me, as sweet as saccharine. I sat down on the edge of the bed, because there wasn't anywhere else to sit. She put out a hand and touched mine. She is the kind of girl who is always touching you. 'That was nice of you, to think of coming to see me.'

I nearly said, 'I didn't think of it, it was Pat Allison,' but I realized this would not have been tactful. Anyway, it was quite likely that Elaine had put Pat up to it.

'Come here, Sam,' she said, and kind of drew my face down, so that I was pretty well obliged to kiss her. That made two girls I'd kissed in three days, if you counted Jenny. But as a setting, a platform on Barhampton Station lacks a certain something, compared with a pretty pink bedroom. When I bent over Elaine, I caught a moist warm whiff of breath and scent and body-smell, all mixed together, that made me feel quite light-headed. Suddenly I wasn't sure I didn't like her after all.

'Congratulations, Sam,' she said softly, 'on your pictures in the *Echo*.'

'Oh, anyone could have done it,' I said modestly.

'Not *anyone*,' she said. 'You had your chance and you took it. I admire that. Have you noticed what's on the wall?'

I looked the way she was looking, and saw that she had a cork board on her wall and my centre-page spread was pinned to it. I'm not easily flattered, but I must admit I felt a bit flattered by that.

'Do you think you'll get more work for the *Echo*?' she asked.

'No, I don't. They told me I wouldn't. I only got that job because of the Plague.' Which reminded me. 'How are you?' I asked.

'Oh, getting better, Sam. Recovering rapidly. *Very* rapidly just now.'

She was giving me eye-signals. I remembered Larry suggesting that perhaps she fancied me. Well, I'd never thought of myself as the Cheltenham type, but a girl could do worse. Much worse.

Then she reverted to the *Echo*. 'Well, even if you don't get more jobs to do,' she said, 'I suppose you've got an *entrée* into the place.'

'A what?'

'I expect you've met people, and you could go there again.'

I thought I was entitled to just a very small boast.

'Well, yes,' I said. 'Ken Edwards — he's the picture

editor — told me to call him by his first name. And he said I could drop in and see them some time, if I rang him beforehand. I only met one of the staff photographers. That was Derek Dixon. The other two were off sick.'

'Derek Dixon,' she said thoughtfully. 'I think I've seen him around.'

'He's very good-looking,' I said.

'Yes, I remember . . . Sam, if you do go into the *Echo* office, could I possibly go with you? Just as a friend?'

I felt a bit doubtful at first. Ken Edwards hadn't said anything about taking a friend. But I looked at Elaine, and I was pretty sure they wouldn't mind having *her* walk into the office. In fact, I have to admit I quite liked the idea of taking her there. A status symbol, you might say. 'Sam Horsfall,' they'd tell each other, 'is the one who took those good pictures for us and has a dishy girlfriend.' Not that Elaine was my girlfriend, but still . . .

'I should think I could fix it,' I said.

'Oh, *Sam*! Aren't you *nice*? Move up this way a bit.'

I edged a little up the bed towards her. Elaine reached out, drew my face to hers, and kissed me. Not just an affectionate peck. A kiss that homed right in on the lips, and stayed there.

'Watch it!' I said, when at last I could come up for air. 'Don't you know, that does something to a chap?'

'What does?' she asked, all innocence. 'This?'

She drew me to her again, and kissed me for even longer. I could feel the tip of her tongue, pushing its way between my lips. Suddenly I was drunk and dizzy and out of control. I was grabbing her, and my hands were wandering in directions I hadn't told them to go.

After about a thousand years she detached herself and pushed my hands away.

'Don't be in such a hurry, Sam,' she said. 'I'm an invalid, remember! And listen. Tomorrow morning, Daddy's coming over to take me home, so that Mummy can cherish me for a few days. I shan't be back until

94

Monday night. But we can go out somewhere on Tuesday. If you want to, of course.'

She gave me a tiny smile. I was floating gently down to earth after the recent high.

'That'll be great!' I said. 'Terrific!'

'I'll ring you from Cheltenham, Sam. You *are* on the phone, aren't you?'

I gave her Auntie's number.

'And talking of the phone, remember to call the *Echo*, won't you?'

11

Jenny

People are changed by what you learn about them. I took a different idea of Sam back on the train with me from Barhampton. Although he'd told me a certain amount about himself, the Sam I knew up to that point was still a Sam who appeared out of the blue and then disappeared back into it. Now I had a Sam in his setting, with his aunt and uncle in the suburban house in Barhampton — and a Sam who had been extended backwards in time, back to his childhood, by the photograph album . He was much more now than a young man who wanted to borrow a camera and take pictures and win a competition. And, knowing more about him, I wondered more. I wondered how he'd liked school and whether he'd been popular with other boys and good at games . . .

And now he was twenty. He must have had girlfriends, mustn't he? A normal young man — and, so far as I could judge, he seemed normal enough — couldn't have reached that age without having girlfriends. But he hadn't mentioned one to me; there hadn't been a picture of him with a girl; his aunt had told me a thousand and one things about Sam but not that.

There were girl students at the Polytechnic, of course. I had a vague idea that the ones in Sam's department would be serious and dedicated, with hands for ever smelling of hypo and no eyes for anything but the composition of a picture. Did I perhaps *hope* they were like that? No, it was ridiculous, I wasn't interested in Sam in that way. His kiss on the platform had been as impersonal as a handshake.

Did I *like* Sam Horsfall, now I'd seen him on home ground? If I looked on it rationally, I wasn't quite sure. He'd been single-minded and a bit ruthless about the Hasselblad, but after all his career was important and I couldn't blame him for taking it seriously, could I? He'd spoken harshly of his aunt, who was kind and warm and in my opinion very nice, but I could understand that in large quantities she might be a bit trying, and in spite of his impatience I thought he had plenty of affection for her. He was blunt to the point of rudeness, and apparently proud of it, and I couldn't myself see that being a northerner was any justification. On the other hand, I was more and more convinced that behind his façade of being a down-to-earth Yorkshireman there was a Sam who was vulnerable and unsure of himself. I wondered again whether it would really suit him to be a press photographer, competing in a tough world where you needed lots of confidence and a thick skin. There was no telling.

Was Sam likely to be thinking about *me*, the way I was thinking about him? No, of course he wasn't. He'd be thinking, as always, about his immediate aims. He'd talked of coming to Kingston, but that was only to bring me the Stratford prints and I wasn't at all sure he would actually do it. I still didn't know why I'd gone to Stratford and to Barhampton for him. Did I have feelings that I wouldn't recognize? Or was I just going round in circles? Did anyone else in the whole wide world become as *confused* as Jenny Midhurst?

I'd brought a novel to read on the train, but I never opened it.

'Well,' said my mother, 'how was the young man today?'

'His name is Sam,' I told her. 'And he's very well, thank you.'

'He made good use of the Hasselblad?' my father inquired.

'Yes,' I said. 'Look.' I took out my copy of the *Barhampton Echo*. 'He took those with your camera. See the credit line? "Pictures by Sam Horsfall." That's him.'

My father took the paper from me, spread it open, and examined the pictures with interest.

'Looks a commonplace job,' he said.

I was surprised by the strength of my reaction.

'Well!' I said, outraged. 'It's the first he ever did, and the newspaper must have thought it was all right, giving it all that space!'

'Cool it,' my father said. 'I didn't mean your friend's photographs. I meant that shopping precinct. Totally ordinary. Anyone in my firm could have done better. As for the pictures, they're competent and they give a clear idea of what it's like. I've nothing against them. Quite the reverse. I respect any job of work that's properly done.'

I'd heard him make that last remark before. It wasn't the highest praise in his vocabulary, but it *was* praise. My father's standards for 'work properly done' were exacting.

'It justifies the lending of the Hasselblad,' he added, with a grin. 'I'm glad to see it working for a living.'

'Is it really only the Hasselblad that takes you all that way, Jen?' my mother inquired.

'It's not a romance, if that's what you mean,' I said.

'By Jenny's account, Emily, she is not the main attraction,' my father said. Then, to me, 'It's time this young man met the Hasselblad's family, however. Otherwise I shall think he's merely trifling with its affections. You must ask him here, Jenny, for a specific day. Preferably a Saturday, when I'm at home.'

Fair enough, I thought. If Sam didn't come, I'd know he didn't really want to see me. If he did come, I'd have another chance to decide whether *I* really wanted to go on seeing *him*.

'All right,' I said.

12

Sam

I walked home dazed from Elaine's flat, still half drunk
with the taste of her lips, and with the scent of her in my
nostrils. With a bit more nerve and a bit less scruple I'd
have made out with her already. I knew it. Even the way
things were, she'd as good as promised . . . Perhaps I'd
been wrong about Elaine. Perhaps I did quite like her after
all. I certainly fancied her.

It wasn't exactly the first encounter of Sam Horsfall
with s-e-x. There'd been Marlene Fisher, back home in
Solomon Street, who went into the park with me after
dusk (and with most of the other lads, too, at one time
or another). She'd introduced me to the basic procedure,
so to speak. I'd thought then it was an overrated pastime.
Well, so it was, with her. And there'd been Dora Steven-
son, after somebody's birthday party: just once, and never
repeated or mentioned again, though Dora was still
around. That was the lot. I wouldn't have claimed to be
experienced. I had a feeling that with Elaine it would be
very different. Deliciously different, as they say in the ads
on telly.

On Saturday afternoon I went to the local shops to get
a few things for Auntie. I thought about Elaine all the way
there and all the way back.

'Sam! Is that you? She telephoned!' called Auntie as I
went into the house.

'Who? Elaine?'

'No, not Elaine! I didn't know you were expecting a call
from *her*!' Auntie's voice took on a coy tone. 'It was

Jenny! She wants you to go over for the day next Saturday and meet her parents. Isn't that nice?' And then, disapprovingly, 'Elaine, indeed! She's never rung here, and I've never met nor spoken to her. What are you up to, Sam Horsfall? Isn't one girl enough?'

'Depends on the girl,' I said, to provoke her.

Auntie looked up at the ceiling. 'What are young folk coming to?' she asked it. The ceiling didn't answer. She turned to me and said, 'When I was a lass, I won't say there was never more than one, but at least it was one at a time!'

'Queen Victoria's dead,' I told her.

'And had been for a good few years when I was born!' Auntie retorted. 'I'm not old-fashioned. But I do have standards. And Jenny's such a *nice* girl. You won't find a nicer, I'll be bound!'

'I know she's nice,' I said. 'I'm grateful to her. But I keep telling you, Auntie, there's nothing more to it than that. Jenny's three years younger than me, and still at school.'

'Three years may seem a lot to you now,' Auntie remarked. 'But in ten years' time it'll be neither here nor there.'

'Ten years' time! For Heaven's sake! In ten years' time I'll be thirty! Are you thinking of *marriage*? Have a bit of sense! Anyway, Jenny lives at Kingston. It's a long way away. I don't think I shall go.'

Auntie looked shattered at that. I was thinking that a long two-way hitch in November wouldn't be much fun. And there was nothing in it for me. I didn't need the camera any more. I was satisfied with my Stratford pictures and confident of winning the competition. And as I'd already done a job for the *Echo*, I couldn't see them denying me the three-month trial that was as good as promised to the winner. All this and Elaine too. Apart from the loss of the Poly's equipment — and surely I was living that down by now — Sam Horsfall was riding high.

'Did you tell Jenny I'd ring her back?' I inquired.

'No,' said Auntie. 'I . . . I . . .' She swallowed. 'I said you'd go.'

'To Kingston?'

'Yes.'

I'd never been so mad with her before. I was wild. Outraged. Furious that she hadn't learned from the previous episode. I actually shouted at her. 'You've no *right*! Whose life is it, yours or mine? I won't bloody well *stand* for it. I shall find somewhere else to live next term!'

There were tears forming in Auntie's eyes.

'I meant it for the best,' she said. 'I told her you'd ring nearer the day to make arrangements.'

'You've no business to tell her anything of the sort! You know what you're doing, Auntie? You're putting me *off* your precious Jenny, that's what you're doing!'

But as I said it I had a sudden mental picture of Jenny's face as I'd last seen it on Barhampton Station. I thought how she'd helped me, willingly, three times, and I told myself, 'You're a rotten bastard, Sam Horsfall!' I didn't want to telephone and say brutally that I wasn't going. As a matter of decency I'd have to go to Kingston, and I'd have to break it to her gently that this was it. I'd thank her for all she'd done, but indicate that there wasn't anything more to do. There couldn't be any future in it.

Auntie was sobbing by now. I put my arms round her, exasperatedly. 'Listen!' I said. 'You mustn't *ever* do anything like this again. Never ever! Promise!'

'Y-yes, Sam. I'm sorry. You won't really look for somewhere else to live, will you?'

'I suppose not,' I said, and sighed.

I wasn't besotted with Elaine. Not a bit of it. I believe in being level-headed and not going overboard about any female. But I admit I thought about her at intervals all through the weekend. I remembered her through my senses, too.

The sight and sound of her I was used to. There never

was any doubt that Elaine Anders was easy on the eye. And although I didn't really like that precise little Cheltenham tinkle of a voice, there was no denying it was sexy. It was the other three senses, however, that kept telling me things. Taste and smell and touch. I could still taste her mouth and smell her scent and her body, and I could still feel on the palm of my hand the smoothness of flesh where I'd slid it down her back and round her haunches. Combined together in memory, my senses were keeping me dizzy.

I had some written assignments to catch up with, but I didn't get on with them very fast. On Saturday evening I went out for a drink with Ian Burns and Ron Spellman, and we had some gloomy talk about the work we hadn't been doing and the poor degrees we were likely to get if we got any at all and the lack of jobs for people leaving college and the miseries of life on the dole. To tell the truth, I didn't really feel all that worried about these matters. Cheerfulness kept breaking in. But I thought I'd better go along with the others, so we all had a good moan into our beer.

On Sunday morning, Auntie Edith answered the telephone and yelled upstairs to me.

'It's the *other one*,' she said as she handed over the instrument. The expression on her face would have curdled milk. This time it really was Elaine, and she tinkled away for several minutes about how Mummy and Daddy were dears but it was terribly dull in Cheltenham and she wished I was there. She made various remarks about the fun we could have been having, which you could take as innocent or sexy according to taste. Knowing Elaine, I took them as sexy. Just talking to her made my flesh tingle. She finished with a reminder. 'Don't forget to ring the *Echo*, will you Sam?' she said.

So on Monday I rang the *Echo*. Actually it wasn't as easy to speak to Ken Edwards as I'd expected. The first two or three times I tried, the *Echo*'s lines were all busy. The next two times, I got as far as the switchboard, but the picture desk was engaged, and apparently remained so until I hung up in despair. Then the lines were all busy again. And when at last I got through to Ken's room, the voice I heard wasn't Ken's. It was that of a harassed sub-editor who was minding the store while Ken was in conference, and who was tetchily convinced that I was somebody called Osborne who'd put some prints on a train from Birmingham.

'Could you ask Ken to ring me back?' I inquired when I'd made it clear that I wasn't Osborne and knew nothing about the prints from Birmingham.

'Listen, chum,' said the voice. 'Ken doesn't ring *anyone* back. He wouldn't ring you back if you were Lord Snowdon. Try again if you like after the last edition time. That's half-past four.' And the voice's owner hung up without wasting time on any farewell.

After that it was a surprise when Ken Edwards did in fact call me back soon afterwards. He seemed much less harassed than his stand-in had been.

'What can I do for you?' he asked.

I told him.

'You want to come and bring a girl, eh?' said Ken. 'Pretty?'

'Yes. Very.'

'Come on Saturday, that's the best day. At noon, when the early edition's gone to press. We'll show your popsie round the paper, and then we'll all go out for a pub lunch. Some of the photographers might come, too. Nothing happens on Saturday afternoon except football, and that doesn't start until half-past two.'

'Thanks a lot, Ken. That'll do fine.'

'Good. See you both on Saturday. Look forward to it. 'Bye, Sam.'

I'm a lucky chap, I thought, as I hung up. I seem to be quite well in with Ken Edwards, and Elaine will be impressed, and if I can meet the photographers as well, that'll be a bonus.

It's not like me to be forgetful, but for once I'd slipped.

It had gone clean out of my mind that Saturday was the day I was supposed to be going to Jenny's.

Elaine reappeared on Tuesday morning and worked beside me at the next enlarger for most of the day. She'd taken a set of still-lifes, all with clever gimmicky lighting, and was busy cropping and blowing-up. She said they weren't entries for the competition, and I believed her. I couldn't imagine that the Director would be favourably impressed by a picture designed to make an apple or half a grapefruit look like an unidentified flying object. But I had to admit it was ingenious.

From time to time she would touch my hand and ask my advice, in a flattering tone, and once she gave me a swift little dab of a kiss while nobody was looking.

'By the way,' she said casually when we were getting cups of tea from the machine, 'I forgot to ask. *Did* you get around to ringing the *Echo*?'

'Yes,' I said. 'It's all fixed up. We're going there on Saturday. A guided tour and a pub lunch.'

That won me lots and lots of Brownie points.

'Sam,' she said, 'you're terrific.' She squeezed my hand. 'Now, what about this evening? *Chariots of Fire* is back at the Regal. Would you like to see that?'

I said I would. I didn't tell her I'd seen it the previous week. Actually it was just as well I had, because Elaine distracted me from it considerably. I dare say playing games in the dark at the cinema is kid's stuff, but Elaine knew a trick or two that schoolkids didn't, or at least they didn't in Bradford in my day.

Afterwards we went to a coffee-bar and I walked her home. Pat and Diane were in the flat, and we drank more coffee and talked. But it seemed that the cinema was my lot for the day. I didn't see the inside of Elaine's bedroom again. At the respectable side of midnight I found myself in the street, heading home for Auntie's.

She knew without being told that I'd been to Elaine's. Her face was drawn up tight with disapproval. But in fact nothing happened during the rest of the week for Auntie to disapprove of. During the day-times Elaine stayed near me and remained affectionate and flattering, but somehow all her evenings were spoken for. On Wednesday she had her domestic chores to do and declined an offer of help. Thursday she was working on a written paper. Friday was one of the evenings when the Department was open late, and she wanted to work some more on her prints of unidentified flying apples and bananas. I stayed on with her, but when she'd finished she said she had to go back to the flat to wash her hair and wait for her parents' regular telephone call. Once again I found myself at the wrong side of her door. It was plain that so far as I was concerned there was nothing more on the agenda until after the *Echo* trip.

As I said, I'd forgotten about the visit to Jenny's home. Auntie hadn't forgotten, but I suppose she was afraid to remind me because of all the fuss I'd made. She didn't know about the *Echo*.

It was Thursday when I suddenly realized what had happened. Larry asked, not very hopefully, if there was any news of the missing equipment. There wasn't, but this made me think of Jenny, and thinking of Jenny brought back to my mind the invitation that Auntie had accepted for me. And it dawned on me at last that there was a clash of engagements.

It didn't take me long to decide what to do. I knew instinctively that Elaine wouldn't forgive me if I cancelled the *Echo*. She wouldn't even like a postponement. And I was reluctant anyway to ask Ken Edwards to change the date. It was Jenny who would have to be let down. I'd have to ring her and make an excuse. And while I was about it I might as well get the whole thing over with and backtrack on the idea of going to Kingston at all. There wasn't room for it in my life.

I'm not proud of that decision. I'd no sooner arrived at it than I felt a pang of regret. I would miss Jenny a little.

I'd quite liked her after all, and now in effect I was about to ditch her. My conscience was going to give me a bit of trouble, and so, in all probability, was Auntie. Well, any reproof would be deserved, and I'd have to put up with it.

I felt a total heel as I dialled Jenny's number.

13

Jenny

I'd been getting uneasy as the days went by and I didn't hear from Sam. My intention in the first place, of course, had been to put the invitation to him directly, not through his aunt. Unluckily I'd telephoned at a time when he was out of the house; and Aunt Edith is amazingly good at taking over a conversation and at finding out what she wants to know.

She was warm and loving and talkative. She thanked me profusely three times over for going to Barhampton and giving Sam so much help. Sam thought the world of me, she said, and her husband liked me too, although being so shy he didn't know how to say it. As for herself, she already thought of me as if I were the daughter she'd always wanted but never had . . . It was a bit much, really, and perhaps a bit alarming, and yet it was enjoyable too to feel her affection lapping around me. It wasn't long before I was telling her the purpose of my call.

'Yes, of course, Jenny love, he'll be all agog to come,' she said. 'I'll tell him the moment he gets in.'

'Hadn't I better ask him myself?' I said.

'He won't *need* asking,' Aunt Edith assured me confidently. 'It's what he's been waiting for. *I* know him. I know him better than he knows himself.' And so on. I didn't feel as confident on this last point as she was.

'Perhaps he could ring me and arrange times and so on?' I said.

'Oh, yes, Jenny love, surely. He'll be glad to have an excuse. I'll tell him to ring you.'

But he didn't. I expected the call all that evening and all the next day and the day after that, and it didn't come. I felt tempted to telephone again myself. But that might seem like pursuing him, and I wasn't pursuing Sam Horsfall. And on previous occasions the silences of Sam had turned out to have an explanation. No doubt there was an explanation this time.

Still, my uneasiness grew. And when I picked up the telephone on Thursday evening and heard his voice, I already had a premonition that something had gone wrong. He sounded agitated.

'This is Sam,' as if I didn't know.

'Hello, Sam.'

No preliminaries. 'My auntie said I'd be coming to see you on Saturday.' A pause. 'Thanks for asking me.' Another pause. I knew what was coming now. 'But' — a third pause — 'well, I can't.'

'I'm sorry, Sam,' I said.

'I've made a prior engagement. I mean, I *had* a prior engagement. I mean, I have to go somewhere else.'

'Oh, that's a shame.' I said. 'Never mind, these things happen. Can we fix some other time? What about the Saturday after?'

'Well . . .' Then he began to hedge. No, he couldn't manage the following Saturday either. As a matter of fact, he was behind with all his work on account of the flu. There were assignments to be finished by the end of term, and he didn't know how he'd ever get through. In fact he wasn't going to be free any time this term.

Perhaps next term, then?

Well, maybe, but that was the busiest term of all. Anyway, there was no point in trying to make arrangements so far ahead. We'd better leave it for now, and if he did get a chance later on he'd be in touch. I half expected him to finish with the classic brush-off: 'Don't ring me, I'll ring you.'

'All right,' I said. I made my voice very calm and steady. 'I see how it is, Sam. I'll wait to hear from you.'

He seemed abashed now. He thanked me for all I'd done. He was sorry he hadn't had a chance to meet my mum and dad. Maybe some day . . .

I felt entitled to be just a bit chilly. 'I take it you don't need the camera any more,' I said. 'Has the lost one turned up?'

'No, not yet. I'll let you know if it does.'

'Oh, never mind,' I told him. 'It doesn't matter in the least.'

I wondered if he ever *would* let me know. I thought probably he wouldn't. So what? I didn't care.

'Goodbye, Sam,' I said; and then, to myself, with silent cynicism, It was nice knowing you.

My father came by just as I put the receiver down.

'Jenny!' he said. 'What are you looking so upset about?'

'I'm not,' I told him. 'By the way, that was Sam. He can't come on Saturday after all. He's sorry.'

'Is he coming some other time?'

'Probably not.'

'Well,' said my father, 'there are as good fish in the sea as ever came out of it. And some of them in less distant waters. Never underestimate the disincentive effects of travel.'

That was his idea of sympathy.

'Thanks a lot,' I said. 'Oh, thanks a lot!'

Not that I needed sympathy. Not really. Well, not much.

Gran and Gramp were on to it at once, though, when I next went round there to tea. I hadn't said anything except 'Hello' and 'What a lovely fire!' when Gran began picking up vibrations.

'Something's gone wrong, dear, hasn't it?' she said.

'No,' I told her.

Gramp was picking up vibes, too. ' "No", meaning "yes",' he said. 'I can read your tone of voice.'

I pulled a face at him.

'There *is* something wrong,' said Gran. 'What is it, I

109

wonder? You're doing well at school, dear, aren't you?'

'Brilliantly,' I said.

'Of course she's doing brilliantly,' said Gramp to Gran. 'She's my granddaughter, isn't she?'

'She's mine too, I'd have you remember,' said Gran. And then, with a little uncanny pounce, 'What happened to the young man who borrowed the camera?'

It was the first time I'd gone to see Gran and Gramp since the Barhampton day. That trip had been on a Wednesday, and the following Wednesday I'd had to go to the dentist after school, so I'd missed two of my usual Wednesday visits and was having tea with them on Friday for a change.

I told them about my trip and about the job Sam had done for the *Barhampton Echo*. Gramp was interested and impressed.

'Why haven't you brought a copy of the paper to show us?' he asked.

'I'm sorry. I forgot.'

'You must be proud of him,' said Gran.

'Why should *I* be proud of *him*?' I said plaintively. 'I don't own him. Anything but.'

'Something's gone wrong between you!' said Gran with certainty.

'Nothing's gone wrong, Gran. There wasn't anything *to* go wrong.'

'*Wasn't!* You sound as if it was all in the past!'

'That's just where it is,' I said. 'Sam was coming to our house tomorrow, and he rang last night to call it off. And I think it's off for good. That's all.'

'Oh, my dear!' said Gran. 'I *am* sorry.'

It's practically impossible to get cross with Gran, but for once I almost managed it.

'There's nothing to be sorry about,' I said. 'He was coming and now he isn't. He used to need Dad's camera and now he doesn't. End of story. It's as simple as that. Now, let's have a go at the crossword!'

'You can make some toast first, Jen,' said Gran. She

gave me a stack of slices of bread and her big old toasting-fork, and I settled on the hearthrug to toast the bread and my face at the open fire. I'd done it a hundred times before, and I felt warm and secure and loved and . . . happy? Why not happy?

When I turned away from the fire, Gran took the toast from me, peered into my face, and said, 'Tears!'

I said, 'Don't be silly, Gran, it's the heat. Everybody knows heat brings tears to your eyes.'

'I've lived sixty-eight years on this earth, and it's the first *I've* heard of it,' said Gran. And, sharply, 'That young man *is* important to you. I knew it.'

'I keep telling you he's not,' I said.

But neither of them took any notice of my remarks. Gramp said thoughtfully, 'Barhampton's fifty miles from here. If a distance like that is too much for him, then he really doesn't want to see you, and you should accept it and be thankful the truth's come out so soon. If a young man is serious, he won't be put off by distance. Eh, Alice?' And he was smiling at Gran.

'Well, *you* weren't!' said Gran. She smiled, too. 'Still, it was *ten* miles, not fifty.'

I remembered something about that.

'He cycled over to see you,' I said.

'That's right,' said Gramp, 'Six days a week I cycled over to see your Gran, when we were courting. The seventh was my day off. And was I ready for it!'

Gran aimed a pretended swipe at him.

'And ten miles then was as much as fifty now,' said Gramp.

'There could be other reasons for not coming, mind you,' said Gran thoughtfully. 'There was a spell when you never came, Leonard. Remember why?'

'No,' said Gramp.

'You haven't forgotten the reason, *I* know. Her name was Harriet.'

'Oh, *Harriet*!' said Gramp. 'She was nothing to me.'

'That's what he's been saying for fifty years,' Gran told

me. She was smiling again; it was ancient history to her. 'But he was taken with her at the time!'

'Fancy!' I said. 'Another girlfriend! I never knew that before! I'm surprised at you, Gramp!' And then, after a pause for reflection, I went on, 'I don't know what girl-friends Sam has. He didn't mention any to me.'

'Your Gramp didn't mention any to *me* !' said Gran. 'I didn't know until long afterwards.'

'And what happened?' I inquired.

'He came back. If he hadn't, *you* wouldn't be here!' Her tone was meditative. 'You see, I was the right one for your Gramp, even if he did stray for a while. These days, it could just as easily be the other way round, or so I'm told. Girls fancy other men, and they've much more freedom than we had. All I'm saying, Jenny, is, don't write this young man off too soon. If he's the right one, he'll be back.'

'And if he doesn't come back, he hasn't any sense and you're well rid of him!' said Gramp.

'I wish you'd listen to me,' I told them. 'There is not, there never *has* been, anything between me and Sam Horsfall!'

'Very well, dear. Just as you say. But mark my words!'

I hadn't convinced her at all. Yet in a strange kind of way I was comforted. If I didn't see Sam again, there was clearly no substance in our friendship. If there *was* substance in it, I would see him again. That was what Gran and Gramp believed, and it made sense.

Gramp had got the crossword out. 'Wickedly at sea,' he said. 'S and five blanks.'

'That's an easy one,' I said. 'Sinbad. Give me another.'

14

Sam

Elaine was ready and waiting when I arrived at the flat to take her to the *Echo*. And she certainly was dressed for the occasion. She'd managed to be informal and sexy at the same time, in a tight new velvety pair of jeans that showed off her neat bottom, and a tight new sweater that showed off her neat top. To walk through the streets, she wore a lambswool-lined windcheater as well, but she took that off as soon as we were in Ken Edwards's little office.

I have to admit I basked in reflected glory. You should have seen Ken jump to attention when she arrived. After that it was a kind of mini royal progress. Heads turned all the time and typewriters halted when he walked her through the big room to see the reporters and sub-editors at work. Then we went down to the composing-room, where somebody set up a headline in large type, ELAINE VISITS THE ECHO, and presented her with a proof of it. There was a distinct wolf-whistle as she left. Then to the process-engravers, which is specially interesting to anyone studying photography, and where she asked all the right intelligent questions. And finally to the machine-room, down in the basement, where the lunch edition was about to come off the presses.

It's quite a moment when the presses start rolling. It carries even me away. Presses so huge there are walkways for getting to the upper reaches of them. A hooter sounding, and the web of newsprint moving slowly forward and halting and moving again, as men with spanners adjust the curved metal plates fixed to the rollers. At last the start of the run, and the presses turning slowly at first, and the newsprint unwinding from reels like enormous toilet-rolls and moving in an intricate pattern through the rollers and along to be cut and folded. The growing speed and noise as the run gathers pace, and more speed and more noise on a rising, exciting note, and the floor beginning to vibrate, and you think the presses can't go any faster than this, they can't they can't they can't they can't go any faster but they do . . . Ken Edwards has his arm round Elaine's shoulders and he's yelling something into her ear but she can't hear him . . . The finished copies are coming off now in rapid serried ranks with the same main front-page headline and picture repeated a thousand times over, and they're heading on a conveyor for the dispatch-room and out to the waiting vans that will whisk them away through the city's midday traffic . . .

By the time we were back in Ken Edwards's little place, the news of Elaine's visit had got around. Two of the photographers, old Tom Sigsworth and young Derek Dixon, were waiting for us there. (The third, Harry Adams, was out of town.) The chief sub-editor, a thin, dyspeptic-looking spectacled man in shirt-sleeves, came in to say hello, and a minute later — but I expect this was coincidence — the editor himself put his head round the door. He was big, portly, red-faced and balding, and he looked Elaine up and down with considerable frankness before inquiring who she was.

'A photography student at the Poly, eh?' he said on being told. 'I'm judging a competition there next month. Are you going in for it, my dear? You are? Fine, fine . . . Well, have a good look at the *Echo* while you're about it.'

'It must be *marvellous*, working here, Mr Dowling,' Elaine said. 'So *exciting*!'

I hadn't known she knew the editor's name. I didn't.

'It's not like the Poly, I can tell you,' Mr Dowling said.

'Nothing academic about this. Damned hard work.' Then, 'I didn't catch your name, lassie. Elaine Anders? Good luck to you, Elaine.'

He went out without showing any sign of having noticed *me* at all. I felt a moment's misgiving. Was I wise to have brought Elaine here? After all, I had my own interests to consider. She was a rival. On the other hand, any prospect of a job with the *Echo* depended on the competition, and Mr Dowling was only one of the judges, and probably they wouldn't know whose pictures they were judging, and anyway why should I suppose that having met Elaine would make any difference to his judgement? I put the misgivings aside.

'Well, now,' said Ken Edwards. 'Just time for a quick bite at the Boar. Come along, people. This way.'

We sat at a bare oak table in a corner of the Boar's Head, eating pub food. Steak pie and chips, apart from Elaine, who had a chicken sandwich and salad. Pints of bitter, apart from Elaine, who had something colourless on ice. Ken paid.

I didn't have much luck with the seating arrangements. Ken and Derek Dixon got themselves at either side of Elaine, and leaned towards her as the centre of attraction. I was the wrong side of Ken, and the only person within talking range of me was Tom Sigsworth. Fragments of the other conversation — mainly the high bright tones of Elaine and her little bubbling laugh — came through to me as I talked with Tom, but I couldn't put the pieces together. It seemed to be largely gossip about the Poly and the *Echo*.

I gave up trying to listen, and turned my attention to Tom. He was a lean, slightly battered-looking man, over sixty but not at all decrepit, and the only newspaperman I've ever met who looked like the public image of a newspaperman. He wore a seedy raincoat and a hat which he hadn't taken off on entering the pub but had pushed towards the back of his head. The only thing missing was a cigarette dangling from the lips. Tom Sigsworth didn't appear to smoke.

'You're retiring next summer, Tom, isn't that right?' I asked him.

'Aye,' said Tom, and supped his beer.

'Will you be sorry?'

'No,' said Tom, and picked up his fork.

'Why? I should have thought you'd miss the life.'

'You can have enough of it,' said Tom. 'I've had forty years. Straight from the Army after the war and never did anything else. It's a job, I suppose. There's plenty that'd be glad of it.'

'Like me,' I said.

'Well, it's all right for a young person. They don't think ahead. Look at Derek there, *he* enjoys it. Dashing around, meeting people, here today and somewhere else tomorrow. But one day you wake up and you're middle-aged and you don't want to spend the rest of your life driving around in all weathers and trying to meet deadlines.'

'It must be exciting, all the same,' I said.

'If it *does* get exciting,' said Tom Sigsworth, 'it scares the pants off you. Like going up in the Pennines looking for cars buried in a blizzard, and getting buried in the blizzard yourself. Or cut off by floods. Or caught in the cross-fire in a strike or a riot. And have you ever thought what it's like to cover a rail or air crash, with bodies strewn around? You need a strong stomach for that.'

Tom was getting warmed up now. He went on, 'And what promotion is there for a photographer? You can be a picture editor, maybe, like Ken. But who wants to be any kind of editor? Stress from morning till night, duodenal ulcers, unhappy marriages . . .'

Ken Edwards looked round. 'Is that Tom moaning again?' he said.

'Just trying to put him off being a press photographer,' said Tom.

'Don't listen to him, Sam.'

'Those that *can* be put off *should* be,' said Tom

sagaciously. 'The only folk that should go into journalism are those that can't be put off by anything anybody says. The rest are better off out of it!'

'There's something in that,' Ken admitted. 'If you can't stand the heat, keep out of the kitchen. But Tom's an old fraud. He's been in this game since before I was born, and loved every minute of it.'

Tom Sigsworth's dour face broke unexpectedly into a grin.

'All right,' he said. 'Well, I tried. But it's true, Sam lad, it gets in your blood. If you're once hooked on newspapers, they never let you go. I wouldn't have done anything else, I admit it. I'm only retiring because I have to. Now, what about another pint?'

'No time,' said Ken. 'Back to work!'

I'd been looking at Derek Dixon and Elaine while Ken and Tom were arguing. Their faces were close together, their conversation animated. I felt a pang of what I suppose jealousy must be like, if you have a jealous nature, which I haven't. I admitted frankly to myself that Derek was good-looking, in a flashy kind of way that I didn't envy but that girls might be taken in by.

We filed out of the Boar's Head, which was only fifty yards from the *Echo* office. I thought Elaine and I had better make our farewells. I thanked Ken for the tour of the paper and for our lunch, and I thanked Tom for his advice, which I hadn't any intention of taking. And I said to Elaine, 'Are you ready now?'

'Sam, dear,' said Elaine, 'Derek's covering the United match this afternoon, and he thinks he could get me into the Press box. And . . . well, we hadn't actually arranged to do anything, had we? You don't *mind*, do you, Sam? I told Derek you weren't the kind of person who'd mind. But of course, if you *do* mind . . .'

'I didn't know you were interested in football,' I said.

'I *am* interested in football, Sam. I'm simply *fascinated* by it.'

'You can come too, Sam, if you like,' said Derek. But

I know when I'm not wanted. Two's company, three's none, and I was the third.

I didn't ring Elaine's number during the rest of the weekend, and she didn't ring mine. I mooched around a bit, and did some work, but not as much as I'd intended. On Monday morning she was there in the Department, as large as life and as sweet as pie.

'Did you enjoy the match?' I asked her.

'Yes, thank you, Sam. It was fun.'

'Who won?'

'Oh, one side or the other, I can't remember which. Or perhaps it was a draw.'

'I thought you were simply fascinated by football.'

'Sam! You sound grumpy! And I was going to thank you for being so civilized. Some people wouldn't have liked my going off with Derek.'

'Some people wouldn't have done it!' I said.

'Sam! You *are* grumpy! Well, I'm very sorry if you were put out.'

I don't believe in beating about the bush. 'Is there any question of *us* going out any more?' I asked.

'But, Sam, we *weren't* going out, were we? We went once to the cinema, but it was because we both wanted to see that particular film. Anyway, you know how it is. Only three weeks of term left, and I'm miles behind with my work. I don't know how I'll ever get all my assignments finished.'

It was almost word for word what I'd said to Jenny.

There's a saying about the scales falling from a person's eyes. I could hear them falling from mine and hitting the ground with a crash.

'Elaine Anders, you're a bitch!' I said. And I added, to myself: Sam Horsfall, you're a proper Charlie. You should have had more sense!

Gossip gets around in our Department. By mid-afternoon, people who'd never known there was anything between

118

Elaine and myself knew that there wasn't any more. It was even known to all and sundry that she'd spent most of the weekend with a press photographer.

As I was getting ready to go home, Tim Weldon came up to me. He was Elaine's last boyfriend but one. I didn't know him all that well. We'd never been pals particularly.

'Come to the Thistle for a drink!' he said. And, when we got there, 'So she did it to you!'

'I guess so,' I said. 'I wasn't in deep, though. Just a toe in the water.'

'*I* was in deep,' said Tim. 'Over the ears. But I'm on dry land now. Join the club, brother!'

'What club?' I asked.

'The H.E. club.'

'What does H.E. stand for?'

'Hate Elaine. What are you drinking?'

We started on pints. Soon afterwards Phil Radley arrived. He was a member, too. We swapped notes about the way Elaine had treated us. Tim said she was exploitative. Phil said she was a tease. I said she was exploitative *and* a tease. By the end of the evening I was sure I was well rid of her.

'I never did like her, really,' I told them. 'It was just an aberration.' They both laughed sardonically.

I'd had a few beers and spent what was left of my grant by the time I got back to Auntie's and my spoiled supper. Auntie was at her most telepathic. She was guessing what had happened within a minute. And I wasn't in the mood or the condition to keep it from her. In fact I let off steam a bit. I even told her about the H.E. club. I have to hand it to her for restraint. She didn't even say, 'I told you so.' (She'd had plenty to say in the previous few days, though, about my desertion of Jenny.) On the present occasion she confined her remarks to the subject of the ruined meal.

I woke early next day with a slight hangover and a very tender conscience. I was thinking that if Elaine was a bitch, there had to be a similar unpleasant word that described *me*. I didn't like myself at all. I thought about

Jenny a lot. I could see her face, rather pale and serious. I could hear her voice, quiet and thoughtful, with none of that tinkly affectation about it. She was worth a thousand of Elaine, or maybe a million. I shook my head, and it hurt.

I would have to put things right with Jenny. If I could.

15

Jenny

'There was a call for you while you were out,' my mother said.

'Oh. Who?'

'The young man with the accent. The one who was supposed to be coming here last Saturday but thought better of it.'

'You know his name perfectly well,' I said.

'Yes, of course. Sam. I was quite surprised. I'd rather gathered from what you said that we weren't likely to hear from him again.' She didn't sound altogether delighted by the surprise.

'Did he leave a message?' I asked.

'No. He said he'd try again later this evening.'

I wished my heart hadn't bumped when Mum mentioned the call. I'd decided that my policy for the future was a calm acceptance that the Sam/Hasselblad episode was a minor and totally unimportant one which was now closed. I wasn't even going to *think* about Sam Horsfall; I would just allow him to sink into the almost forgotten past. And now . . . Well, I wasn't going to telephone *him*, that was for sure. I was clear in my mind about that.

An hour later he was on the line again. This time I answered the call myself.

'It's Sam.'

'Hello, Sam.' I wasn't going to help him out. 'I didn't expect to hear from you again.'

'No. Well.' I could hear the embarrassment in his voice. 'Things have changed.'

'You mean,' I said coldly, 'that you do need the camera after all?'

That was a shot in the dark, and it didn't actually hit the target. But I was sure it made him jump.

'No, I don't!' he said, instantly and emphatically.

'Then why are you ringing?' I asked, still coldly.

'I wanted to make things right, that's all.'

'I didn't know they were wrong,' I said.

'I mean, well, I'd like to see you. And you said I could come some other time, I wondered if we could fix it.'

'I thought,' I said, 'that you were busy, now and forever after.'

'I . . . Well, like I say, things are different. I'll tell you when I see you.'

I hesitated. It was on the tip of my tongue to say, '*If* you see me.' But I told myself, Don't be stiff and proud, Jenny Midhurst. And my heart was bumping again.

'Oh, hell, Jenny,' he said. 'I *want* to see you. Will you or won't you?'

I swallowed hard. I heard myself saying, 'Yes, Sam.' And a few minutes later, to my father's sardonic amusement and my mother's apparent dismay, the arrangement was on again. Sam would come over on Saturday, one week late.

'I knew he'd be back!' said Gran triumphantly. 'Bring him here for tea!'

'And tell him to bring some prints,' said Gramp. 'I'd like to see what he can do.'

'You mean you'd like to show him what *you* used to do!' said Gran to Gramp, severely. 'You're getting to be a dreadful bore in your old age!'

Gramp winked.

He was right on time. Twelve noon exactly. He'd come by train, to avoid the risk of not getting a lift, and I gathered later he'd hung around for twenty minutes, not wanting to be early. I answered the doorbell and he stood there, grinning uncertainly. He seemed just a shade *smaller* than he'd looked in his aunt's little house. He had a large envelope in one hand and a bulging plastic supermarket bag in the other. He handed the bag, with some embarrassment, to my mother. It was a gift of currant buns from Aunt Edith, who apparently was convinced that southern women were no good at baking.

I wasn't surprised that Sam looked unsure of his reception. I hadn't made any attempt to sound overjoyed on the telephone, and I'd guessed previously that he was a bit apprehensive about meeting my parents. He needn't have worried about my mother. For better or worse she was taught good manners as a girl and has been controlled by them ever since. I sometimes wish she would fly off the handle and shout or swear at somebody. It would do her good. As it is, you can always rely on her. She was totally charming, and received the buns with cries of surprise and delight.

My father is much less predictable. He takes to people or doesn't take to them, and either way he makes no attempt to conceal it. And I should have warned Sam about the handshake test. Dad is not particularly macho, but he does have this conviction that any man worthy of the name must have a firm masculine handshake, and he tests new acquaintances with his own vicelike grip. I watched with some concern as Sam, having disposed of the buns and transferred the envelope from right hand to left, entered innocently upon the ordeal. But it was clear in a moment that he wasn't being outgripped. In fact some kind of contest was taking place. The two of them grinned at each other and squeezed away. After half a minute my father retrieved his hand.

'You have a good grip, Sam Horsfall,' he said. 'Have a drink.'

That was a promising start. And they went on as they'd begun. My father is a naturally argumentative man. He doesn't mind too much which side he takes, so long as it produces a good knock-down scrap. He expresses socialist views to conservatives and conservative views to socialists. He can find a hundred arguments against nuclear missile bases, and just as many in favour of them. If he can shock the person he's talking to, he enjoys himself even more. He took Sam out to walk in the garden while my mother busied herself with the lunch; and by the time Mum sent me out to join them, having made very little use of my offer to help, they were going at it hammer-and-tongs. Sam doesn't have Dad's capacity for taking either side at will, but he's absolutely convinced that whichever side he takes is right. He stood up vigorously for his opinions. To my father this is the intellectual equivalent of a firm handshake. Sam was still doing well.

And so to lunch. My mother sat quietly observant. Dad wouldn't have noticed if Sam ate peas with a knife or picked up his soup bowl and drank from it. Mum would have taken note of the tiniest social indicators. I thought she probably had Sam precisely docketed already. After the meal, Dad took Sam into the kitchen to help him wash the dishes. (Washing-up after meals is my father's bit of male non-chauvinism, and he makes quite a production of it.)

We could hear their raised voices coming out of the kitchen. Dad had got on to the subject of arranged marriages, which he was stoutly and provocatively advocating. (My mother, silent on the sofa, looked at me and raised her eyebrows. Their own marriage had been in the teeth of opposition from her family.) Sam said arranged marriages were no doubt all very well among the wealthy and aristocratic to whom marriage was merely a contract for the disposal of assets. My father, still provocative, asked whether Sam included *him* among the wealthy. Sam drew attention to Dad's professional success, comfortable house and large garden, and said he did. My father pounced. He told Sam delightedly that he had a huge overdraft and the house was mortgaged to the hilt. Further, he said that Gramp had been an ordinary country boy and that he himself had gone to the local primary school. He gave Sam to understand that we were descended from a long line of landless labourers. (Mother, whose two grandfathers were a brigadier and a bishop, raised her eyebrows again.)

'I keep looking at that envelope,' she said a little later. 'Are there photographs in it, Sam? Do show us.'

Sam had brought the Stratford prints and two big blow-ups of Susan on the railings. Not trusting his memory, I'd telephoned the previous day and reminded him. I'd also asked him to bring some examples of his work at the Poly to show Gramp when we went to my grandparents' house in Richmond for tea later on. There were a few of my own Brighton and Stratford pictures, too, but Sam carefully set them apart from his, and made it clear that they weren't his responsibility.

My father studied Sam's pictures with close attention. 'Well composed,' he said. 'Technically excellent. Totally without imagination.'

'Robert!' protested my mother. 'Really!'

'I am praising him,' said my father. 'Imagination is a greatly overrated quality. There is too much of it around. I see my distinguished colleagues putting up buildings that look interesting but don't do the job, and I wish they had far *less* imagination.'

I've heard him say on other occasions that any fool can design a building that stays up, but what's really scarce is visual excitement. The opposite view entirely. My mother raised her eyebrows yet again. 'Robert,' she said, 'you are showing off. Stop it. And it's a beautiful day. I'm sure Sam and Jenny would like to go out.'

My father agreed at once. 'And I expect,' he added to us, 'you'll want to take the Hasselblad.'

Sam muttered something about not having a film. I suspected he was without the money to buy one. But Dad removed any fears. 'I put a film in it last week,' he said, 'and used half a dozen frames to photograph the site of a house I'm designing. You can use the rest and develop the film. It's HP-4. Fair deal?'

Sam brightened and assented to the bargain. I put my coat on and waited while he visited the bathroom.

'He's very nice, dear,' my mother said. 'Something of a rough diamond, perhaps, but I like him.'

'He'll do,' said my father.

That was high praise.

The river was the obvious place to go; and, as we were due at Gran's and Gramp's house for tea afterwards, we took a bus to Richmond, where the riverside walking is good.

I love the river. One of my daydreams is to have a river-bank house with a broad green lawn sloping to the water and a boat moored at the end of it. There's never a dull moment with the Thames. There are the lovely sights like sails and swans; and at Richmond and below there's the everyday to-and-fro of river traffic, from rowboats and little put-putting affairs through river police patrols and snazzy expensive launches to working barges and sometimes an ocean-going vessel. There's the river itself, different every hour of every day with changing weather and the state of the tide, and the endlessly varied scenery along the banks.

I have a favourite line of poetry about this river, and I quoted it: 'Sweet Thames, run softly till I end my song.'

'Say that again,' said Sam.

I said it again.

'Who wrote it?'

'Somebody called Edmund Spenser.'

'A southerner, I suppose. Still, it's not bad. Not bad at all. Mind you, the Aire at Leeds is quite something.'

Sam was thoughtful for half a minute. Then he said, 'This chap Spenser. He wasn't as famous as Shakespeare, was he?'

'Well, no.'

'Pity. A line of poetry and a river scene might have made a good entry for the competition.'

'That's a good idea, Sam. Why not try it?'

126

'I think Shakespeare has the edge, really. Being the top name, and with the Stratford architecture as well. Still . . .'

For the first time, I got the impression that Sam might just possibly be a little less than totally satisfied with his Stratford pictures. I was all in favour of his trying again. But by now it wasn't such a brilliant day after all. It had been sunny earlier on; but it was late November, and now in mid-afternoon the light was fading and mist was thickening over the water.

We used up my father's film, all the same. Sam took a lot of pictures of boats and bridges. I got my hands on the camera for long enough to photograph a colony of house-boats, desolate in the mist, and a pattern of reflected light in the water. Sam observed these exercises indulgently. And there was a surprising moment when I was gazing out across the river and he called, 'Jenny!' I turned towards him. Click.

'That's the first time you've thought *me* worth a frame,' I said.

Surprisingly, Sam looked embarrassed.

With the film finished and the light now failing fast, we sat for a few minutes on a bench.

'Now,' I said. 'Tell me what happened. Why couldn't you come last week, and why *can* you come this?'

Sam looked uneasy. 'I arranged to go and visit the *Echo* last Saturday,' he said. 'I forgot about coming here. And I thought they mightn't like it if I messed them around.'

'So you thought you'd mess *us* around instead?' I said.

'No. I mean . . . well, it might have been difficult to fix a different date.'

'That's all right, Sam,' I said. 'I understand.' Actually I only partly understood. I could see that he mightn't want to change his date with the *Echo*. I couldn't see why he'd told me he was booked up for ever after, more or less, and had then found he wasn't. There had to be some other explanation. And into my mind from nowhere in particular came the recollection of Gran reminding

Gramp that at one time he hadn't been seeing her because of some mysterious person called Harriet.

'Sam,' I said on impulse, 'there are girls in your department at the Poly, aren't there?'

I thought he jumped. 'Yes,' he said. 'There's as many girls as chaps. About twenty of each.'

'And is there one who's a special friend of yours?'

That was cheek, of course. Cheek, and also instinct. I've never known what made me say it, and I wouldn't have done if it hadn't been for some kind of sixth sense. Anyway, Sam positively blushed.

'No-o,' he said, in an uncertain tone which told me that, though maybe not actually lying, he had, so to speak, something to declare.

'There is, isn't there?'

'There was. Sort of. For a little while. Not now.'

'What's her name?'

'Elaine.'

I felt — there was no mistaking it — a little stab of jealousy.

'Is she pretty?'

'Yes.'

Another stab of jealousy, quite a sharp one. I told myself it was ridiculous.

'Are you fond of her?'

'No, I hate her.'

That was better. At the same time, it sounded rather odd. I just looked at him.

'Oh, well,' Sam said. 'I might as well tell you. Where I come from . . .'

'We believe in being frank,' I said. 'Blunt. Straight from the shoulder. Come on, then, Sam lad, let's be having it.'

This time *he* gave *me* a look. Then he grinned, still uncertainly, and told me. It seemed that this Elaine had practised a few time-honoured wiles upon him in order to get him to take her to the *Echo*, whereupon she'd promptly transferred her attentions to a photographer: to the very photographer, in fact, whom Sam and I had

128

watched at work, and who, I must admit, had struck me as rather dishy.

Sam's account of the episode was full of explanations of how he wasn't susceptible to feminine charms and wasn't easily taken in. It seemed to me to demonstrate that he *was* susceptible and *was* easily taken in, and that the outcome served him right.

'What if she fell out with the photographer and started making eyes at you again?' I inquired.

'There'd be nothing doing!' said Sam with emphasis.

I wondered. I felt a bit uneasy about Elaine, even though I hadn't heard of her until a quarter of an hour ago, and even though I still kept telling myself that Sam's affairs were of no concern to me. When he told me a minute later of the Hate Elaine club, I surprised myself by offering to be enrolled as a member.

He rather liked that.

'You know,' he said thoughtfully, 'if somebody had told me a couple of years ago that I'd ever have anything to do with folk from places like Cheltenham and Kingston, with fancy houses and well-to-do parents, I'd have told them not to be so daft. It's surprising what a chap can find himself doing.'

'You mean you're being corrupted by the South of England?' I inquired.

'Well, I wouldn't say that, exactly.' And then, in the tone of one making a major concession, 'I suppose it takes all sorts to make a world.'

'Even Cheltenham and Kingston?'

Sam grinned.

'Come on,' I said. 'It's getting dark. Let's be on our way. Gran will have the chocolate cake waiting.'

We continued along the towpath. When Sam drew my arm into his, I half-disengaged myself and said, 'I haven't forgiven you for the Elaine episode yet.' But a minute later our hands seemed to wander together, and found each other.

'However, I *might* forgive you,' I said. 'I'm considering it.'

129

16

Sam

There are some folk that have closed minds. They know what they think about everything, and they never change. Well, I'm not one of them. Where I come from, adaptability is the price of survival. I reckon to be flexible. And there are times in life when you can see you've been getting things wrong. That week — the tenth week of the autumn term at Barhampton Polytechnic — was a week of sorting things out, for me.

Sam's Week of Enlightenment, Jenny called it afterwards. She would.

First there was the Elaine episode. Not that I really learned anything new about Elaine. I'd always known what she was like. There's no more point in complaining that Elaine uses chaps for her own purposes than there would be in complaining that a cat chases birds or a snake wriggles. It's the nature of the animal.

But I could see that I'd been soft in the head myself. It should have been clear to a child of ten, never mind a grown Yorkshireman, that she wanted to get her foot in the door at the *Echo*, and I was her means of doing it. I wondered whether Derek Dixon too was just being used and would eventually qualify to be a member of the Hate Elaine club. Well, I wasn't going to worry about that. For the moment no doubt Derek was congratulating himself and probably feeling grateful to *me*. Good luck to him.

Then, I could see Jenny was right in saying I'd been hard on poor Auntie. True, she'd driven me up the wall with her inquisitiveness, but she did mean well and, although her efforts on Jenny's behalf had been counter-productive, I was more and more sure she'd got Jenny right. As for myself, I hadn't so much got Jenny wrong as not got her at all. She'd kind of come along with the Hasselblad as part of the package deal. I hadn't seen the individuality of her. I'd hardly even noticed the things I was beginning to like rather a lot: the dreaminess, the way she made strange remarks out of the blue or came up with sudden lines of poetry, the *Jenniness* of her.

It was meeting her Gran and Gramp that opened my eyes, really. We went to their house from the riverbank, and I took to them at once. Gramp, small and thin and wiry with thick white hair, quick in his movements and sharp in everything he said, and still a bit of the bright little boy in him. Gran, equally small, quiet, but not at all soft or dim, and having him just where she wanted him. I bet he'd been steered by her every day of his married life and never realized it.

And for both of them the sun shone out of Jenny's eyes. Maybe that's a thing about grandparents. I mean, your parents have to take you for granted a good deal, the way you do them, but to your grandparents you're always special. They loved her, they really loved her.

It was while I was there that I started having new thoughts about the pictures I'd been taking. I've always been set against an arty approach to photography, and I still am. I'm not a fancy kind of person. It's always seemed to me that a camera is there to record what's in front of it. Of course you choose what you'll point it at, and you try to compose a good picture, but the real concern of photography is with subjects, not with shapes and patterns, and still less with making things look like what they aren't.

We spread all our pictures out. Mine, Gramp's, and the few of Jenny's. Mine were the best technically; no doubt about it. Gramp, fifty years ago, hadn't had lenses as good as we have now. Jenny's shooting was haphazard and her focus and exposure were often not quite right. And yet, looking at them all together, I found myself feeling defensive.

Maybe, in a contradictory kind of way, the remarks of Jenny's dad were affecting me. If a hundred people had *complained* that there was no imagination in my pictures, I'd have told them where to go. But when this one man actually praised my Stratford shots for lack of imagination, I was inclined to sit up, take notice, and wonder what was wrong. ('I like your dad, and we get on fine, but he's an awkward cuss,' I told Jenny once. 'So are you, and that's why you get on fine,' said Jenny.)

Anyway, although neither Gramp nor Jenny made a comment of this kind, I felt a need to justify myself. 'A camera's a reporter,' I said, picking up my old theme. 'I believe in accurate reports, not vague or misleading ones.'

'Yes, a camera's a reporter,' Gramp said mildly. 'But it doesn't just report what it sees. It reports the photographer as well.'

And I realized at once that he had a point. You could tell from his pictures that the young Gramp had been an idealist, a romantic. You could tell that Jenny's view of things was personal, affectionate, and highly visual in a quirky kind of way. As for mine . . . would you suppose that Sam was the kind of person who took pictures like that? Exact, reliable, a bit flat-footed . . .?

Unfair, my soul cried out. That's not *me*. There's more to Sam Horsfall than that. I'll have to think about it all some more.

There was one particular picture of Gramp's that specially seemed to make his point. A study of a young woman. I knew it was Gran, because Jenny told me. It was a loving portrait, and one that cast light both ways, so to speak, because there was something about the eyes and lips from which you could tell that the photographer meant as much to the subject as the subject did to the photographer. My eyes kept going back to it. I think I'd have guessed it was Gran anyway; I could see so much of Jenny in her.

132

We put the prints away and had tea. There wasn't actually any chocolate cake. It was hot-buttered toast and home-made scones and jam, and we stayed talking far too long. When we left I got a kiss from Gran and a handshake from Gramp that was nearly as sinewy as his son's, and they waved to us from the doorway as if we were off to Australia.

When we were round the corner and out of sight, I looked at Jenny and she smiled and said, 'Aren't they nice?' I said, 'Aren't *you* nice?' and I was kissing her, on the lips, not at all in the way I'd done on Barhampton station. She could tell the difference, and her body was tense, and it was dark and getting chilly and certainly not a bedroom scene, and there were no scents or smells except fresh air, but her lips were very willing and I was liking her and she was liking me.

We'd promised to go back to Kingston, but by the time we arrived there wasn't time for much more than 'Hello' and 'Goodbye'. Jenny's parents invited me to come again. I said I'd love to. Whether or not this meant anything I just didn't know. I'm not an expert on the folk-ways of Kingston-upon-Thames, Surrey. In Bradford, if we said 'Come again' we'd mean 'Come again', but in Kingston, for all I knew, it was just a form of words and might merely mean they hadn't hated you enough to throw you down the front steps.

Her dad had been hyping up his handshake, and this time he got a quick advantage and won the contest, but I managed to grin cheerfully and show no sign of the agony he was inflicting, which went some way towards keeping level. Her mother shook what was left of my hand, coolly and formally. It would be quite a while, I reckoned, before she matched Gran's spontaneous kiss. Then, as we were on the very point of leaving, Jenny said, 'Hey, Sam, what about taking out the film? You're going to develop it, remember.'

So I opened up the Hasselblad. And immediately I saw that I wasn't the only forgetful person in the world. There

133

was another right here in Spinney Lane, Kingston, Surrey. Jenny's dad had told me the camera was loaded with HP-4, and I'd been judging the exposures accordingly. Well, it wasn't. It was FP-4, which is much, much slower. So the film would be hopelessly under-exposed, and there wasn't a cat-in-hell's chance of getting a decent picture off it. (I did get it developed at the Poly later, but it was useless, as I'd expected).

I'd found Robert Midhurst rather alarming, but I felt sorry for him over this disaster. His face was red as he apologized. Actually I didn't mind all that much; the light had been poor and I doubted whether I'd got anything particularly good. I quite enjoyed being gracious and forgiving, and putting myself at a moral advantage for once.

Time was even more pressing now, and Jenny hurried me to the station. We got there just before the train came in.

I said, 'I'm not sure I'm quite happy with the Stratford pictures as my competition entry after all. What about coming with me on another expedition?'

Jenny said, 'So you're *still* after the Hasselblad!'

She was teasing, so I said, 'Yes, of course, I always have been!' And then, more seriously, 'There isn't much time. Entries have to be in by Monday week. Still, it'd be fun if we could go off somewhere for the day again, just the two of us.'

Jenny said, 'You mean, just us and the Hasselblad.' But then she smiled and went on, 'Yes please, Sam, let's. Where shall we go?'

I hadn't thought about that, and the train was just arriving at the platform. There was only time for a snatched kiss, and I was on my way.

I considered the next trip all the way back to Auntie's. The picture reports the photographer, Gramp had said. Interesting. Perhaps the trouble with Stratford was that it wasn't really *me*. To Sam Horsfall, Yorkshireman, it was foreign territory. And so, for that matter, were Brighton and the River Thames at Richmond. I didn't know them in my bones. Maybe I should go to my own county and see if I did better there.

I still liked the architectural idea, though. In my own county I'd surely find architectural subjects with beauty and character. Where? Well, it wasn't long before the answer came to me. Where else but York itself? I'd gone to York, on and off, ever since I was a little lad. I knew it well and was at home there. I would take Jenny and the Hasselblad to York. I thought happily of that prospect the rest of the way to Barhampton, in between blessing Derek Dixon for removing Elaine from the scene.

I got back to Auntie's to be greeted with a shock. She told me there'd been four separate telephone calls for me, all from people at the Poly. One was from Tim Weldon, two were from students I was on good terms with but who weren't special friends. And one was from Larry Lomas.

Hmmmph, I thought. Something's up. I felt a shade apprehensive. I decided I'd better go to the horse's mouth and ring Larry. He and his wife Sheila have a kid of about two and another on the way, so they're not going out an awful lot at present, and it was Larry himself who answered the phone.

'Sam!' he said, 'I have good news for you. Have you seen this week's *Amateur Photographer*?'

'No,' I said.

'Listen to this, then. It's in the small ads, between vivacious nude models and the adult slides for sale. "Will the young man who left photographic equipment in a green Cavalier car at Brighton on 17 September telephone the following number, identifying himself and the equipment?" '

For a moment I was taken aback and couldn't say anything.

'That has to be you, Sam!' Larry went on. 'Obviously the stuff's safe. All's well that ends well. Aren't you going to cheer?'

135

'Yes,' I said faintly. 'Terrific.' I still couldn't quite take it in. I'd got so used to the load on my mind from losing that equipment that it was hard to believe it was rolling away.

'Here's the number. You'd better ring it right away, Sam. It's somewhere on the south coast, I think. And go and collect the equipment as soon as you can. Take a day off if necessary.'

So, a couple of days later, I was hitching south once more. And that day I added an extension to the Horsfall Theory of Hitching. The new clause says there will be just one day in the year when everything goes in your favour. Then you have it made. You won't have to wait a minute before you're picked up and taken exactly where you want to go at high speed by delightful people.

That's how it was for me. I got lovely rides in both directions. The chap who'd driven off with my gear was very decent and even gave me lunch. He'd had to go abroad and then he'd had flu, which was why he'd been so long in doing anything about it. I staggered back into Auntie's the right side of midnight, tired, but carrying the Poly's Hasselblad and the rest of the stuff, complete and unharmed. And there was a cheque waiting for me, from the *Echo*, for my pictures. It was bigger than I'd expected. Sam, lad, I told myself as I crawled into bed, your ships have come home. Tomorrow you'll be able to look Larry and the rest of them in the eye again. And when you make that trip to York you'll have the Hasselblad with you. You won't need Jenny's.

That last thought gave me a jolt. Could I ask Jenny to go all the way to York when I didn't need her dad's camera? The question was still in my mind when I woke up next morning, and I pondered it at intervals at the Poly, where everybody congratulated me on the recovery of the missing kit. Somehow I was only giving two cheers instead of three.

Of course I could go to York without her. But the moment of truth had arrived. I didn't want to go without her. I didn't even want to *risk* going without her.

I thought she liked me, but still, it was a long way to go. Maybe to her, and even more to her parents, I was just that young man from the North that she'd been willing to help out. Now the need was over, they might all think there was no reason why she should trail around the country with me any more. After all, during the Elaine episode I'd thought there wasn't a future in knowing Jenny. Why shouldn't she and her parents think the same about knowing me?

No, I said to myself, I won't take any chances. I'll ask her to come to York and bring her dad's Hasselblad just the same. I won't tell her the other one's been found.

I was a bit shocked by my own decision. I've always reckoned I'm a straightforward kind of chap. No deceit in me. 'Tell the truth even if it hurts,' and so on. But, well, all's fair in love and war.

War? There certainly wasn't a war on.

Love? That word startled me. A dangerous word. Look out, Sam, I said to myself. Watch it. Take care.

But I still wanted Jenny Midhurst to come to York with me.

17

Jenny

Susan had a boyfriend. She'd acquired him somewhere around half-term, and she talked about him non-stop at school. His name was Andy, and we gathered he was so handsome that girls swooned at the sight of him. He worked in the local building society. Susan had met him when she went to pay in her birthday money. Apparently it had been love at first sight across the counter, and they were now going out regularly together. It gave Susan great pleasure to explain that she couldn't go anywhere with me any more, because all her free time was taken up with Andy. She gave me to understand, however, that if I had a boyfriend as well we might be able to make up a foursome now and then.

'Not that there's much sign of it yet, is there?' she said sweetly.

I hadn't told her about my last two encounters with Sam, but on the Monday after his visit I gave her the two big prints of herself against the railings. She was as pleased with those as ever.

'Andy will be interested,' she said. 'He's a photographer, too.' And then, generously: 'Why don't you come to tea and meet him?'

So I did. I admit I was curious to see what Andy was like. After all the build-up I half expected he'd be a weedy, pimpled youth. Actually he wasn't bad-looking: fairly tall, with curly almost-black hair. He was wearing a dark business suit, white collar and discreet tie, and carrying a neat executive briefcase, but I suppose he could be forgiven all that because he'd come straight from work.

I didn't *like* him much, all the same. He was condescending about the picture of Susan when he learned that I'd taken it.

'Not bad,' he said. 'Of course, being *contre-soleil*, it could have done with a stop more. But I've seen much worse.'

Susan, who had begun by boasting about the picture's merits, now back-pedalled smartly and excused its deficiencies, pointing out that I was only a beginner.

'Andy has such high standards,' she said. 'He's *very* good. Almost professional, aren't you, Andy?'

'I do my best,' said Andy modestly.

Then Susan began to tell the tale of the seaside day that had produced the picture. I thought at first that Andy was bored by it. But when she came to the subject of Sam he perked up and showed interest.

'Left his camera in a car?' he said. 'At *Brighton*? Hold on a minute.' He dived for the smart executive briefcase and opened it. There was nothing inside but a copy of *Amateur Photographer*. Andy riffled through the small-ad pages at the back, and finally thrust something in front of us.

'Will the young man who left photographic equipment in a green Cavalier car at Brighton on 17 September telephone the following number. . . ?'

'Is *that* him?' Andy demanded triumphantly.

Well, of course, it had to be Sam. I was elated at first. I knew how much the matter had weighed on his mind. It would be an enormous relief for him, and I would enjoy breaking the news. I told Andy and Susan truthfully that I couldn't remember Sam's telephone number but I had a note of it at home, and I undertook to let him know. I thanked Andy effusively on Sam's behalf.

And then on the way home I began to wonder. What about the trip that Sam had proposed? When he recovered the Poly's Hasselblad he wouldn't need my father's. He might give up the idea of the joint expedition. And I knew from the dull cold thud with which this thought dropped into my mind that that was the last thing I wanted.

I told myself to be sensible. It was my obvious duty to give Sam the news at the first possible moment.

But . . . after all this time, would a few more days' delay make any difference? Couldn't I give him the news in person when we met? In the meantime the camera was safe, and nothing could go wrong.

Of course, it was highly possible that he would see the ad himself, or that somebody else would show it to him.

But no, apparently not. He telephoned the following night. My heart gave a little skip when he announced himself, and another when he proposed that we should go to York on Saturday. I'd never been to York in my life. It was a long way away, but the trains from London were good and fast and I could get a cheap-day ticket. Suddenly the world was an exciting, fascinating place, and it was wonderful to be alive, and the one thing I wanted above all else was a trip to York with Sam.

'And . . . the camera?' I asked.

'You can bring it, Jenny, can't you?' he said.

'I expect so. Yes, I'm sure I can.'

'That's good. How could I manage without you? I mean, without it?'

It took me about half a second to dismiss my remaining scruples. We talked about train times and arrangements to meet, and I didn't say a word about Andy's discovery. That ad in *Amateur Photographer* might never have been.

18

Jenny

So we are in York, or perhaps we are just outside it, for we are facing the turreted gateway of Micklegate Bar, with its great arch astride the traffic-laden street and its lesser arches at either side and the city walls stretching away from it in both directions. I've never been here before, but I've read about it, because I'm the kind of person who always does read about things first, and I know that the city is three-quarters circled by its walls, and that the walls are punctuated by these great gates or Bars at points of entry, and the River Ouse flows through the middle of it from Lendal to Skeldergate bridges, and over it all within the northernmost bend of the walls presides the Minster.

I know all this, which is not to say that I know anything about York. I know a little more when I stand at Micklegate Bar and feel that it's the entrance not just to any old city but to a city of pride and presence, an important city, a capital city.

Sam's feelings are obviously less exalted than mine, but he seems to know a few of the gorier bits of York's history. 'They used to stick traitors' heads up there,' he says. '*That* taught 'em a lesson.'

'A bit late, I should have thought,' I say, and giggle; but I can imagine all too clearly the sightless, decayed, once-living faces, and a shudder goes down my spine.

It's December now, and blustery, and there won't be much daylight, and we have work to do. So we're up on the walls in no time, first looking down on handsome

Micklegate as it curves broadly away to the right, and then putting our heads down and pushing westward against the wind, and I am buttoning my raincoat for warmth and to prevent it from becoming a sail and carrying me off the wall and down the perilous steep slope of the inner rampart. Then we turn north, past the long curving roof of the railway station, outside and below the walls on our left. Now the wall begins to undulate and we're heading slightly downhill and suddenly there's a distant view of the towery Minster and the wall snaking ahead of us towards it. Sam is stopping and bending over the Hasselblad and taking a lot of care to get his exposure right, and I am rubbing my hands together and stamping my feet and giving him a well-meant but half-frozen smile when he looks up for a moment. Then we're on our way again, arm-in-arm now and almost heeling over from the force of that wind, and I'm happy and at home in it like I suppose a bird is at home in the sky.

And so across Lendal Bridge, with views up and down the wind-ruffled river and a few hardy anglers braving it out on the bank, and we are picking our way through the Museum Gardens to see a corner of the old Roman wall, rather small-scale and rough-looking and altogether upstaged by the splendours of the later ones. It occurs to me that the medieval walls which I've been thinking of as old are actually the *new* ones.

'Bit scruffy, isn't it?' says Sam of the Roman wall, unimpressed, but I've read *The Eagle of the Ninth* and I'm remembering that York was the headquarters of the Ninth Legion, and a few years after these walls were built the Legion marched north to deal with an uprising and was never heard of again. Another chill down the spine.

Steeply up on to the walls again at massive Bootham Bar, where you look on the outward side over broad open spaces and big handsome buildings but on the inside you're jostled by a humbler, pleasant mixed jumble of shops and houses on High Petergate. And then a lovely stretch past the elegant houses and gardens of the Minster

Yard, and we're walking all round the Minster at a distance, raised high above ground level, with constantly changing views of its intricate, complicated shape. Sam is taking picture after picture, but I notice that he has time to look down from the Minster and focus on a trio of gardeners raking leaves to feed a fire whose smoke swirls wildly in the wind. Maybe his ideas are changing.

The sun is making fitful appearances now, shining for odd minutes through breaks in the scudding clouds, and when we reach the northernmost corner of the walls and Sam wants to take a southward-looking picture, he's worried by sunlight falling on to the lens, and has me shelter it with my hand. We're very close now, and when he's finished Sam pushes the camera aside and draws me towards him and we're pressed together in an embrace, our bodies a centre of warmth against the cold surrounding air. We stay like that while the sun goes in and comes out and goes in again.

On again, past the north side of the Minster and the conical hat of the Chapter House, with views across gardens through the bare branches of trees. I suggest shots to Sam, and sometimes he tries them and sometimes he doesn't, but he's using quite a bit of film and putting exposed reels into a little black bag like a sponge-bag. Houses bobbing up in the foreground now as if determined to get into the picture, and then Monk Bar ahead and Sam is leaning perilously over the outer parapet and trying to get a shot from an impossible angle of what looks like a heraldic beast on the outside of the gate.

'Watch it!' I urge him. 'That's my dad's camera you're risking, as well as your neck!' Sam pulls a face like a gargoyle and leans out even farther. If I could turn him to stone he'd be an interesting addition to the architecture. But he gets his picture and wriggles triumphantly back to safety.

This is the opposite gate from Micklegate and we've come half-way round the city, but now we finally leave the wall down a little steep stairway. We pass the Minster without going in, because there won't be all that much light today and we need it outside. And now we're making our way through a web of crowded narrow streets, through Low Petergate, and the Shambles where the upper storeys face each other so closely that you can imagine people shaking hands across the street, and Pavement, and the Market, and Davygate and delicious pedestrian Stonegate, and buildings of every style and century huddled together in rich profusion and confusion and Sam taking shot after shot after shot and people people people people and my mind is reeling backwards and forwards through the ages.

We eat in a self-service place that just happens to occupy a building that's hundreds of years old and has floors at odd levels and exposed beams and mysterious corners in which you can find a table to take your pizza to. Then into the streets again, heading for the Minster, which in a strange way has dominated everything even when you couldn't see it. The west front is huge and mixed and assertive and there's too much of it, and I'm sobered up a bit by not liking it. But inside, startlingly, the wind roars through the nave, and I am going wild again, for I have an absurd feeling as if we were in a vast stone ship at sea, a high and noble ship, sailing in search of some immortal destination . . .

Come off it, Jenny, I tell myself; calm down. A kindly patrolling clergyman has been reading my face — am I so obviously starstruck, I wonder? — and is leading me towards the Chapter House, with a bemused Sam trailing behind. But first we must pass the Five Sisters window, with its bleak, immensely tall panes of grey-green, geometrically-patterned glass in which there is no picture; and the cold austere light that comes through on this December afternoon makes me think of a different eternity in which there is no life and the planets turn pointlessly for ever in space.

That's not the Minster's last word, though, and in the Chapter House I believe in life again. The Chapter House is circular, and the high arched windows that reach up all round to the vaulted ceiling are full of light and colour and tracery and as large as they could possibly be and separated only by slender columns, so it's almost as if you were in a dome of coloured glass. I come to earth to find the kindly cleric watching my face and beaming as if he'd invented the whole thing for my benefit, and he murmurs a Latin tag which he tells me means 'As the rose is the flower of flowers, so is this the house of houses.' Or possibly, he says, the dome of domes, for the Latin word is the same. But that is outside my learning.

Sam comes and takes my arm and says, 'Jenny, love, it's time we went for the train.' I go without a word of protest, because I'm filled to the brim with this city and I can't take any more. But later, when the train is sliding southward and outside the carriage window it's all dark and Sam is asleep and I'm awake with my head on his shoulder, I don't know how much of the day's happiness was York and how much of it was being with him, and it doesn't make any sense to separate the causes.

19

Jenny

Sam was awake when the train drew into King's Cross station, and looking at me in an odd, guilty kind of way. And that look reminded me of something. I had a confession to make.

'Sam,' I said, 'there's something I have to tell you.'

'There's something *I* have to tell *you*,' he said.

'You go first.'

'No, you go first.'

I took a deep breath.

'There was an ad . . .' I began.

I caught his eye, and before I could finish the sentence I *knew*.

'. . . in *Amateur Photographer*,' he said.

We both giggled.

'Will the young man . . .' I began when I could get the words out.

'Who left photographic equipment . . .' continued Sam.

'In a green Cavalier car . . .'

'At Brighton on 17 September . . .'

We couldn't get any farther. We were helpless with laughter. People in the carriage were staring at us, then some of them smiling and even laughing in their turn.

'You didn't need me at *all*,' I said when I could get myself together.

'I didn't need the Hasselblad,' Sam corrected me.

I got home rather late, very tired, and very happy. My

mother recognized the happiness as well as the tiredness. I must have been radiating it.

'I don't need to ask if you've had a good day,' she said.

I just smiled.

'Come and tell us about it.'

My father was in the drawing-room, sipping his bedtime whisky.

'So it got back safely,' he said, referring to the camera. 'I hope it liked York.'

'It loved it,' I said. 'So did I.'

'I think you liked your company, dear, didn't you?' my mother said archly. A few weeks ago that remark would have made me cross, but not now.

'Yes, I did,' I said shamelessly.

'Tell us.'

'About the photography,' said my father.

So I told them how the day in York had gone, leaving nothing out but the embraces, which I considered my mother could imagine for herself and my father wouldn't think of. I got more and more carried away as I moved in recollection round the city. When I finished, my father was thoughtful and silent for about half a minute. Then he said, 'Jenny, without further evidence I will buy you any camera you like.' And to my mother he said, 'This girl has possibilities. I am entertaining a dreadful thought. What if she were to become an architect?'

Then the telephone rang. I went to it. Sam. He hadn't got as far as his aunt's. He was calling me from the station. He told me why.

'Oh, *no!*' I said. 'Oh, Sam, you *couldn't!* Not even *you!* What *will* you do now?'

He'd lost the little black bag with the exposed films in. He didn't know where he'd dropped it. It could have been in the Minster or on the station or in the train, but most likely it was in the streets of York. Wherever it was, there wasn't a hope of getting it back in time to make prints for the competition, which closed on Monday morning.

'Did you ever hear of such a chapter of accidents?' Sam said. He sounded desperate. 'I don't know what to do.'

'You'll have to enter the Stratford pictures,' I said.

'I won't do that. They're not *me*. I mean, they're not me *now*.'

There was a brief silence. Then, 'Jenny, we're in this together. I can't manage without you. Will you come here tomorrow? To Barhampton? Please? We'll take what pictures we can around the place in the time we have. I'll develop them in Phil Radley's darkroom in the afternoon and hand in an entry on Monday morning. We'll just make it!'

'And you said you'd go?' my mother said, 'just like that?'

'Yes,' I told her. 'He needs me.'

'I think,' said my father to me, 'that you should consider the possibility of finding a less disaster-prone young man.'

'*I* think,' said my mother to him, 'that your daughter is in love.'

I said, to both of them, 'Boo!'

20

Sam

She brought it again. Her dad's camera, I mean. I'd returned the Poly's Hasselblad to base and hadn't asked for it for the York trip, so I didn't have it that weekend anyway. I was furious with myself about the York pictures and Jenny was rueful, but there was one compensation for the loss: it gave us a day together we wouldn't have had. It was a fine day, too. A good day, even in Barhampton.

Compared with York or Stratford or Brighton, Barhampton isn't much of a place. It's flat, in every sense of the word. A railway town with big repair shops from the age of steam, now run down. A carpet industry, ditto. A modern attempt at recovery, with an industrial estate of low, flat-roofed factories and warehouses, about as elegant and homely as a deserted airfield. A dozen or so busy streets in the city centre, with the usual main-street stores that might be anywhere in the United Kingdom. A canal running grimly through the older industrial area. Miles and miles of dreary suburbs. And of course the Poly and the shopping precinct that I'd photographed, and the *Echo*.

We passed the camera back and forth between us, taking lots of pictures. Sometimes the same subjects, from different angles and distances. Sometimes different subjects that appealed to one or other of us. I soon lost track of who'd taken what. It didn't seem to matter. We took a lot of pictures of corny old buildings that wouldn't have dared raise their heads in Brighton or Stratford, but had a kind of dilapidated charm. Lots of pictures of the canal, which when you come to look hard at it isn't ugly; it's beautiful in a strange, sad way.

Pictures of children playing, squabbling, running, roller-skating or just fooling about among all this ungrandeur. Lads kicking a ball around. Men waiting for a pub to open. Dogs around a dustbin. Women gossiping. Somebody pegging washing across the street. A man's legs sticking out from under a car. An angler fast asleep under his umbrella. A picture of Jenny by me that she didn't know about. Two pictures of me by Jenny that I only knew about when I developed them. Pictures, pictures, pictures.

We went home to Auntie's for midday dinner, rather late. Brisket of beef and Yorkshire pudding, the real thing. Uncle Frank came in from fishing, ate his meal, surveyed Jenny in a wondering kind of way as if a creature from outer space had paid us a return visit, remarked after much thought that it was a nicer day than last time she was here, and went back to his fishing. After dinner I took Jenny to Phil Radley's, and we developed the films and printed everything that looked possible. We dried off the prints with a hair-drier. I had dreadful doubts about them. A few weeks earlier I wouldn't have looked at any of them twice.

We took them back to Auntie's and spread them out on the front-room table. Auntie's general view of pictures taken by me is that they must be brilliant because *I'm* brilliant. She looked uncertain about some of these, though. They were decidedly lacking in roses-round-the-door appeal.

'What happened to the Stratford ones?' she asked.

'And the shopping precinct ones?' asked Jenny.

I said I had prints of all of these in my bedroom.

'Bring them out,' Jenny said.

So we spread them out with the rest. The more I looked at the Stratford pictures, the more I was disappointed. THIS IS STRATFORD-UPON-AVON, they were telling you. A

LEADING TOURIST ATTRACTION. BIRTHPLACE OF WILLIAM SHAKESPEARE. THE BARD. But, as Jenny had said, he wasn't there. Nobody was there. The Stratford of the pictures was dead, not to say embalmed.

The shopping precinct ones were just a shade more interesting. At least they were less familiar than the sights of Stratford. They were a decent professional job. I'd done them for money and I'd earned what I was paid. Nothing wrong with that. Among them was the one taken at the foot of the broad curving ramp to the upper level, with the little shambling old man looking around him in elderly bewilderment. He was still on this print, though the retoucher had wiped him off the one that appeared in the *Echo*. Illogically, something inside me gave a tiny cheer. The poor old sod had not been totally done away with after all.

Finally there were the Barhampton ones. To be honest, they were rough and ready. They'd been taken hastily, developed and printed hastily. Technically they weren't all that good. But there was life in them. People being themselves and doing things. There was something to be said, of course, for putting a picture of Barhampton on a calendar issued by Barhampton Polytechnic. But the glories of Barhampton were non-existent. I couldn't really see the Director being impressed by a pair of size ten boots sticking out from under a Morris Marina.

I kicked myself again and again for the disaster of York. *That* would have been a winner. Real people, a real place, real visual excitement, and I'd let the whole lot go down the drain. Auntie and Jenny had refrained from saying anything to me about it. But I hadn't refrained from saying things to myself. Rude ones.

Jenny said suddenly, 'Let *me* choose the entries, Sam.'

I was startled. I'd assumed all along that *I* would choose the entries. Of course I would. It was *my* future that was involved. I might listen to what she said; I might even listen a tiny bit to what Auntie said. But it was up to me to decide. I wouldn't trust anyone else to do that.

Or would I? I thought about it hard. Jenny had been right about a lot of things. Perhaps I could trust her. Perhaps I would even *prefer* to trust her . . .

'Then I can share the blame if you don't win,' she said.

I made up my mind.

'You're not taking any blame,' I said. 'That's *my* privilege. But you *can* choose. I'll leave you to it. There's an envelope in that drawer. Pick three prints, put them in it, seal it, and address it to Larry Lomas marked "Calendar Competition". And don't tell me what you've chosen, because I'll only start arguing if you do. And then come into the kitchen and we'll all have a cup of tea.'

At one minute to nine on Monday morning, I handed the envelope to Larry. He put it on top of a little pile. There seemed to be about twenty entries. All sealed, of course.

I told him about the York disaster. Larry sighed.

'Oh, Sam, Sam!' he said. 'You'd lose your head if it was loose!'

'Is there an entry from Elaine?' I asked.

'Yes, of course there is. She's crazy to win.'

'What has she put in?'

'I don't know, Sam. I told you all at the start, I wasn't going to look at your entries, and I've stuck to it. I don't know what anybody's done. And any minute now the Director's secretary will collect them and take them from the envelopes and number them. So they'll all be anonymous. The judges won't know who took what.'

'I dare say *you'll* know,' I said. 'You've seen lots of everybody's work.'

'Maybe, maybe not,' said Larry. 'Anyway, there are four other judges. *They* won't know.'

Anne came in then. She's the Director's second secretary. (He's so important and busy he has to have two of them.) A little blonde piece. Tap-tapping on high heels. 'Hello, Larry.' Hands stretched out for the envelopes. 'Hello, Anne. Here they are.' 'All complete, Larry?' 'As

complete as they're going to be. I won't accept any more.'
'OK, Larry. Byeee.' Tap-tapping out again.

'Well, that's it,' Larry said. 'In the lap of the gods now. Or demigods, maybe. The Director, the Dean of Visual Studies, the Dean of Architecture, and George Dowling from the *Echo*. To say nothing of yours truly. Judging this afternoon at three.'

He added ruefully, 'Trust you to bugger things up for yourself, Sam Horsfall. I hope you found something good after all.'

And I knew he'd have liked me to win.

At least we weren't going to be kept waiting for the verdict. It was to come straight after the judging. I suppose that was because of Mr Dowling. They couldn't expect a busy man like the editor of the *Echo* to trot over to the Poly twice.

We gathered in the auditorium at four. It was pretty full. There were only two more days of term, and a lot of people in various departments had finished their classes and hadn't anything better to do.

The contestants were there, of course. Elaine was with her flatmates, Pat and Diane. She was laughing and chatting, and looked perfectly relaxed. Not all tensed up like me. My heart sank as I looked at her. Maybe she was confident she'd got it all sewn up. Maybe her confidence was justified. Larry had said she had imagination. Jenny's dad had said *I* hadn't.

I sat about as far away from her as I could get, between Tim Weldon and Phil Radley. The Hate Elaine club, out in force. Elaine caught my eye from right across the auditorium and gave me a little wave. I scowled back.

They were late starting. Anne, from the Director's office, came tripping on stage at five past four to a mixture of cheers, boos, hisses, applause and wolf-whistles, and announced that the judges were still deliberating. Another five minutes passed, and another. A few people got tired of waiting and trickled out. It was nearly twenty past four when the judges appeared. A table and five chairs were waiting for them, centre-stage. The Director led the way, but pulled out a chair deferentially for Mr Dowling, who was the visiting Big Wheel. They sat in the middle, flanked by the Deans of Architecture and Visual Studies, with Larry, very much the junior member, at outside left.

The Director got up and gave an introductory spiel. He's a tall, well-built, handsome man with a tanned face and crisp, curly grey hair. Wears beautiful suits. Lots of presence. That's what got him the job, say those who don't like him, but there's no doubt he looks good beside Mr Dowling, who is equally tall but bulging at the midriff, balding, and generally going to seed.

Anyway, the Director apologized for the delay and said it was an indication of the high standard of the work submitted, and how impressed he and his colleagues had been. The competition, as we would all recall, was entitled 'The Eye of the Beholder', and he was glad to say that the contestants' eyes had been beholding what was around them to some purpose. Blah blah blah.

Then the Director reviewed the entries in general. He'd been fascinated to see that there were several nudes. (Cheers.) Obviously some very interesting work was being done by members of the Photography Department. (More cheers.) Unfortunately, though any of these would have resulted in a decorative and no doubt highly popular calendar, he didn't think Barhampton Polytechnic was quite the right organization to publish it, and he recommended them to try elsewhere.

At this point Mr Dowling intervened and said he might buy some for the paper in case they started a Page Three glamour feature. This was baloney, designed to get a cheap laugh, because the *Echo* is a respectable provincial paper and would lose half its readers if it ever published a nude. The joke fell a bit flat.

Anyway, said the Director, there'd also been landscapes and seascapes and portraits and still-lifes, all of remarkably high quality, and the judges were very sorry they couldn't give a prize to everybody. Blah blah blah again.

He now came to the winners. I sat up straight. They'd awarded the third prize to Ian Burns, who'd submitted three excellent wild-life pictures, from which they'd chosen one of a squirrel on a stump holding some delectable morsel between its paws. Well, well, well. Big deal. Ian Burns had been boasting all term about his new zoom lens, and it had paid off, in a tiny way. Five pounds for Ian. Hardly worth the trouble. Larry held up the picture, but of course nobody in the hall could see from a distance what the hell it was.

The Director teased us all with the second prize. He didn't immediately say who'd won it. This contestant had had the excellent idea of photographing people at the Poly going about their daily business. One picture, he said, had been of himself at his desk, and he was sorry that his well-known modesty forbade its use on the Poly's calendar. (Laughter.) Another was of students eating and chatting in the cafeteria. The judges had liked that very much, but the one they'd chosen as second-prize winner was of members of a life class drawing from a model who, the Director hastened to add, was adequately clothed.

The second prize went to Elaine Anders.

I was really surprised now. I hadn't thought that kind of thing was in Elaine's line. She'd gone out of her way to avoid the clever-clever approach that we all thought of as her trademark.

However, was second prize good enough for Elaine? Twenty pounds couldn't matter to her; what she wanted was the job. I looked across the auditorium and saw that she was smiling happily. If she was disappointed, I had to admit she was managing not to show it.

Then the Director came to the first-prize winner. My heart was pounding now and my palms sweating. Obviously I was first or nowhere. What if I was nowhere?

The first-prize winner, said the Director, like several other contestants, had chosen Barhampton for a setting.

(*Several*? So that didn't tell me much.) Of the three entries, one was a lively glimpse of children at play. (Well, that might be mine and might not. I'd taken several such pictures, and so perhaps had other entrants.) Another showed a line of anglers on the canal bank. (I was holding my breath now. That could be mine, too; but it wasn't impossible that somebody else might have chosen it.)

The third and winning picture, said the Director, was a superb illustration of the theme 'The Eye of the Beholder'. Not the beholder *of* the picture, the beholder *in* the picture. Barhampton was rightly proud of its modern development, but there were some, the survivors of a bygone age, to whom these splendours could bring only bewilderment; and this baffled response to our brave new world has been caught precisely (the penny dropped with a crash like thunder) in the winning picture by (but there was no suspense now) Sam Horsfall. Sam Horsfall won the first prize of fifty pounds, and his photograph would be featured on the Polytechnic calendar.

Larry held up the picture of the tottering old man in the shopping precinct. People in the front row got up and crowded round to see it; nobody else had a chance. The Director beckoned me on to the platform. He was shaking hands with me. Mr Dowling was shaking hands with me. Derek Dixon had appeared from nowhere and was taking charge of the proceedings. 'Just a step forward, Director, please. Mr Dowling, could you go to Sam's other side? Now, if you'll draw together so I can get you all in . . .' A cheque was handed to me three times before Derek was satisfied and the smaller cheques could be presented without much ceremony to the runners-up.

Nobody mentioned that my picture in its altered form had appeared in the *Echo*. Did nobody realize? Surely Larry did? But if he did, he wasn't saying anything.

'Well done, Sam,' said the Director when it was all over. 'Well done, Sam,' said Mr Dowling, glancing at his watch and getting ready to leave. 'Well done, Sam,' said the Deans of Architecture and Visual Arts, all matey. 'Well done, Sam,' said Derek Dixon. 'Be seeing you.'

Elaine was there too. 'Congratulations, Sam,' she said softly, touching my hand, Elaine-style. Not a sign of jealousy in her. Had I got Elaine wrong? I didn't know. I didn't know anything. I was in a total whirl. I shook about fifty more hands. Somebody reminded me to pick up the cheque, which I'd left lying on the table. I reeled away from the auditorium towards the pay phone in the corridor outside.

21

Jenny

I was just home from school and taking off my coat when the phone rang. It was Sam, and he could hardly get the words out.

'We won!' he said. 'We won!'

'The competition?'

'Yes, of course the competition. We won!'

'Terrific!' I said; and then, 'Which picture?'

'The little old man.'

I was exultant. 'It deserved to,' I said. 'It's a marvellous picture. Congratulations, Sam.'

'*You* chose it,' he said. 'How did you know it would win?'

'I didn't. I thought it had a chance, that's all. I knew *you* wouldn't enter it.'

'No, I wouldn't have done,' Sam said. 'There must be a moral there somewhere.'

'There is,' I told him. 'Always trust your Jenny.'

'I guess so. Jenny, love, I couldn't have won it but for you.'

The glow from that was just beginning to spread deliciously through my body when the pips went for the end of the call.

'I haven't got another coin,' said Sam.

'Give me the number, quick, and I'll call you back.'

'Don't bother just now. I want to get round to the *Echo* office before Ken goes home. Jenny, I've got a job! A job! And listen, I want to tell you something. I . . .'

But the line was dead.

22

Sam

The presses were thudding with the last edition when I went in at the side door of the *Echo* office. The editorial floor was almost deserted. In Ken Edwards's little room there were pictures strewn everywhere as usual, but Ken had turned his back on them and was just putting his coat on.

'Hello, Sam,' he said.

'Hello, Ken. Heard the news?'

'I've heard a lot of news today, Sam. We deal in the stuff.'

'I mean, about the photographic contest.'

'Oh. Yes. Mr Dowling just looked in. Derek's picture wasn't in time for today's paper, but it'll be in the early edition tomorrow. A picture with the editor in it always gets in.'

'I won, Ken!'

'I know, Sam. Congratulations.'

'So I'll be joining you.'

There was something about his expression that I ought to have noticed before.

'Sit down, Sam,' he said, sweeping pictures from a chair on to the floor.

I sat down. There was a hollow feeling in my stomach.

'Sam,' said Ken Edwards, 'I told Larry I hoped to give the winner a three-month trial. I said it in good faith. Tom Sigsworth's retiring next summer, and I thought it would be up to me to find the replacement. But, Sam, the operative word was "hope".'

He was embarrassed now.

'Go on,' I said.

'I don't have the power of hire and fire, Sam. Only the editor has that. He doesn't *have* to act on my advice. When it comes to the crunch, he can do what the hell he likes.'

'And?'

'Well, you know Elaine Anders, Sam. Of course you do; you brought her here in the first place. She's going around with Derek Dixon now. And she's been in and out of the office a good deal lately. Sam, *she* wants the job.'

'I know she does.' And then it burst out of me. 'Bloody hell, you mean you're taking *her* on instead of me!'

'Mr Dowling says so.'

'Elaine! Bloody Elaine! Why should *she* get it? No, don't bother to tell me. It isn't *what* you know, it's *who* you know. She's wormed her way in all right!'

'It's not that, exactly, Sam. Elaine has imagination . . .'

'She hasn't a monopoly of it!'

'And she has lots of initiative'.

'She certainly has!' I agreed grimly. 'I know *that* to my cost. She has a pretty good figure, too. I bet that didn't do her any harm!'

'I think Mr Dowling quite likes the look of her,' Ken admitted. 'But she'll be all right in the job. Sorry, Sam, but there it is. You can tackle him about it if you like, but I'm afraid you won't get anywhere. The editor's decision is final.'

23

Jenny

He telephoned again the same night. I was reading
Persuasion in my bedroom. For once, my father
answered the phone.

'It's your admirer,' he told me.

I'd been wondering at intervals all evening what Sam
had been on the point of saying when he was cut off.
Could it possibly have been what I thought it might have
been? Well, if it was, he'd say it again, surely.

But he didn't say anything again. What he had to tell
me was new. Bloody Elaine had got the bloody job. And
so on, in language that didn't shock me but would no
doubt have startled Miss Austen.

I did my best to lead him down gently from his heights
of sound and fury. And gradually he got calmer and more
coherent.

'Sam,' I said eventually, 'are you sure it was what you
really wanted?'

'The grapes are sour, you mean?'

'Not that exactly. But do you want to spend the next
forty years taking pictures of Barhampton bigwigs?'

'No, of course I don't. Neither does Elaine or Derek
Dixon. But it's a start, Jenny. And anyway, dammit, it's
a *job*. Hasn't anyone told you, jobs are scarce? Half our
graduates from last year haven't got one yet.'

It was a long conversation. I did my best to persuade
him that he'd find a job. There were still two terms to go,
and some said the market was improving. And he was
good, wasn't he? Yes, he said, he was good, but there

were plenty of good people on the dole. Well, didn't winning the competition count for anything? Not much, he said. And didn't Larry like him, I asked? Hadn't Larry helped him before, and wouldn't Larry help him again? There were limits to what Larry could do, he said, and added bitterly, 'As has just been demonstrated.'

But I was quietening him down all right. After a long time I dared to remind him that there was something he'd wanted to tell me earlier on, before we were cut off.

'Oh. Yes,' he said. 'About your Gran and Gramp. I've got a present for them.'

I'd thought it might be something more personal to me. But if so he'd forgotten in his anger and excitement. I didn't want to sound disappointed. And I was pleased that he'd had Gran and Gramp in mind.

'Are you going to tell me what the present is?' I asked.

'No, it's a surprise.' A pause. Then, 'I'd like to give it to them in person.'

That was good, anyway. 'No problem,' I said. 'They're always at home. Come as soon as you can.'

'My term ends on Wednesday. I'll be going north at the weekend.'

'Mine ends on Thursday.'

'I'll come on Friday, then, if that's all right. With a bit of luck I'll be able to borrow Uncle Frank's car. He often gets a lift to work on Fridays. And I'm rich, since the *Echo* paid me. I can afford the petrol.'

He was asked to lunch, of course. My mother was sympathetic when I explained how he hadn't got the job, though I think she found it hard to believe that anyone could actually want to work for a newspaper, except perhaps *The Times*. My father was thoughtful.

'Friday,' he said. '*I* could be home to lunch on Friday. There's something I'd like to talk to that young man about.'

And in due course Sam arrived, in a small elderly Ford. My father was waiting for him, with his handshake at the ready, but Sam was prepared for it.

'Pax!' said my father after a few seconds. Sam released him, grinning.

In half a minute's time they were out in the garden, locked in verbal combat. I left them to it. Dad had rearranged his day on purpose, and that couldn't be bad. And over lunch he became serious.

'Listen, Sam,' he said. 'My practice is a big one. Eleven partners. Heaven knows how many jobs we have on hand at any given moment, to say nothing of prospective jobs that don't come to anything. And they mostly call for camera work of one kind or another.'

'Oh?' said Sam.

'What do you think I have a Hasselblad for? Just for lending to people who leave them in cars?'

Sam said nothing.

'But my partners and I have other things to do besides taking photographs,' Dad went on. 'Some of us aren't very good at photography anyway.'

'You mean you forget what film you've put in the camera?' inquired Sam innocently.

My father roared with laughter. 'One to you, Sam Horsfall!' he admitted. Then, serious again, 'We've been thinking for some time about taking on a professional photographer. Do you find that interesting?'

'Yes,' said Sam.

'Are *you* interested in it personally? As a job for yourself?'

'Well, I *would* be,' said Sam.

'Never mind "would be", Sam. *Are* you?'

'I would be if it wasn't you, Mr Midhurst.'

'What the hell do you mean by that?'

'I mean, if you think I want to get a job through knowing Jenny, you've another think coming. *I'm* not bloody Elaine.'

My father said, with heavily controlled patience, 'I'm not offering you a job because you know Jenny. I am offering it to you because it needs doing and you are properly qualified for it.'

163

'No, thank you,' said Sam.

My father exploded.

'Sam Horsfall,' he said, 'you are a pig-headed Yorkshireman and I'm not going to argue with you. You don't *deserve* to get a job!' He turned to me. 'Why,' he demanded, 'do you have to take up with a person suffering from galloping integrity? Probably terminal integrity, in fact. He'll never survive in this wicked world!'

'It's just the way he *is*, Da,' I explained.

'Well, you'd better get to work on him,' my father told me, 'and the sooner the better.' I could tell his exasperation was subsiding. 'Let me know if you change your mind,' he said to Sam. 'And in the meantime, good luck to you!'

He stretched out his hand. Sam wasn't prepared for it this time. Father won.

'Ow!' said Sam.

'Serve you right, you arrogant sod!' said my father delightedly.

Sam's uncle needed the car in Barhampton after work, so Sam had to get it back there quite early. There was just time to call on Gran and Gramp. It was a bumpy ride in the ancient vehicle, and I was glad to arrive. Sam stopped the car in the street outside Gramp's house, but I didn't get out at once.

'Sam,' I said plaintively, 'you haven't kissed me today. Not once.'

'I'd better do something about that,' he said, and did. It lasted quite a while.

'You do it nicely,' I said, slightly shaken, when we came apart. 'Where did you learn?'

I could have sworn he blushed. He changed the subject.

'You understand about that job with your dad, don't you?' he said.

'Not really, Sam. It sounds a good job and, as he says, you're qualified for it. Why not take it?'

'It wouldn't do for you to be the boss's daughter.'

'Oh, *Sam*! I wouldn't be the boss's daughter. I'd be Jenny.'

'It's no good,' he said decisively. 'Not my style.'

'My father's quite right,' I said. 'You *are* a pig-headed Yorkshireman. I seem to like you like that, don't I?' I sighed. 'Anyway, you're not taking the job, or so you say. I *shall* have to work on you, if I get the chance. Where do we go from here, Sam?'

'I don't know, love. Just for now, I'll be heading north. Christmas in Bradford with about a million relatives. You can't imagine it. Now, where did I put that present for your grandparents? It's not like me to . . .'

'Lose things? Oh yes it is! If that flat packet's the present, it's in the glove tray.'

24

Sam

They were glad to see us, all right. Well, I suppose it was mainly Jenny, but still, they made me welcome. I got a great hug and kiss from her Gran and a wiry handshake from Gramp. (It must run in the family.)

And of course the package drew their eyes. Jenny made the announcement. 'Sam's brought you a present!' she said. 'And *I* don't know what it is!'

All three of them were agog. They clustered round. I put it in Gran's hands and she fumbled with it. I could see that Gramp and Jenny were all impatience to grab and open it, but they left it to her. And at last she got it out.

'Why, it's . . .' began Gramp.

'It *isn't* me!' Gran declared sharply. 'It's Jenny!'

And it was. It was one of the pictures I'd taken of her at Barhampton. I'd made an oval cut-out that masked everything but the face, and then I'd blown it up big and printed it in sepia and mounted it, so that it looked just like Gramp's photograph of Gran all those years ago. He positively ran to fetch his own picture and put them side by side.

I won't say the likeness was uncanny, but it was even more striking than I'd remembered.

'She's changed a bit since then,' remarked Gramp. Tactlessly, I thought, but Gran didn't mind. And Gramp went on, 'Still, I dare say Jenny'll wear just as well as her Gran.'

'Honestly, Gramp!' Jenny protested. 'You make us sound like pieces of furniture!'

Gramp winked. Gran went bustling off, making tea and toast, and I left half an hour later than I'd intended, which meant that unless I put my foot down Uncle Frank was going to be tetchy by the time I got back to Barhampton. But then, I liked that old pair. When I left, they thoughtfully withdrew from the doorway so I could say goodbye to Jenny. But I'd kissed her properly in the car, and we both felt a bit of awkwardness now. So it was just a little peck, like on Barhampton station.

Well, that's it, I thought. Barhampton today and Bradford tomorrow. In spite of all the ups and downs it's been a good term. Thank you, Jenny.

25

Jenny

I stood beside Gran, drying the dishes as she washed them. Gramp had gone to fetch coal from the bunker outside.

'Such a *nice* young man!' said Gran. 'You're so lucky! And of course *he's* lucky too.'

But a lump was coming in my throat. I couldn't say anything.

Gramp mended the fire and came through to wash his hands at the kitchen sink. He looked pleased with himself.

'Jenny,' he said. 'I've had an idea. You're always saying you don't know what to give us as presents. Well, why don't you take a picture of Sam for us? A companion-piece to his picture of you!'

'What a lovely idea!' said Gran. 'The very thing!'

And then I found myself sobbing. I couldn't help it.

'How c-can I?' I demanded. 'I've just said goodbye to him. We haven't arranged anything. F-for all I know, I'm never going to see him again!'

They wouldn't believe it. They stared at me. I mopped my eyes.

'Like to bet?' said Gramp. 'I'll offer you ten pounds to a penny that you see Sam Horsfall again. And many more times than once!'

'That's right, dear,' said Gran. 'Your Gramp only bets on *certainties*. Of *course* Sam will be in touch with you soon. You mark my words!'

26

Sam

I drove for about a mile, and stopped. It's not like me to forget things, but . . .

27

Jenny

The telephone rang.

'It can't be you!' I said. 'You only left here five minutes ago!'

'I'm in the nearest call-box.'

'What's the matter? Have you left something behind? I *bet* you've left something behind!'

'I haven't, Jen. At least, I don't think I have. Listen, I've just remembered. About the pictures of York.'

'What about them?'

'There was some good stuff there. We'll have to go and take them again next term. You'll come, Jen, won't you? Hell, you *must* come. I *need* you.'

'Oh, I expect I'll come,' I said. 'I always was a soft touch.'

'Right. That's fixed then. I'll have it to look forward to, all through Christmas. Goodbye, Jenny love. See you.'

I turned from the phone to find that Gran and Gramp had come up behind me. They didn't say a word. They just stood there gloating, hand in hand, like a pair of naughty, knowing children.

Other great reads ✦ *from* **Red Fox**

Further Red Fox titles that you might enjoy reading are listed on the following pages. They are available in bookshops or they can be ordered directly from us.

If you would like to order books, please send this form and the money due to:

ARROW BOOKS, BOOKSERVICE BY POST, PO BOX 29, DOUGLAS, ISLE OF MAN, BRITISH ISLES. Please enclose a cheque or postal order made out to Arrow Books Ltd for the amount due, plus 30p per book for postage and packing to a maximum of £3.00, both for orders within the UK. For customers outside the UK, please allow 35p per book.

NAME _____

ADDRESS _____

_____

Please print clearly.

Whilst every effort is made to keep prices low, it is sometimes necessary to increase cover prices at short notice. If you are ordering books by post, to save delay it is advisable to phone to confirm the correct price. The number to ring is THE SALES DEPARTMENT 071 (if outside London) 973 9700.

Other great reads **from Red Fox**

Leap into humour and adventure with Joan Aiken

Joan Aiken writes wild adventure stories laced with comedy and melodrama that have made her one of the best-known writers today. Her James III series, which begins with *The Wolves of Willoughby Chase*, has been recognized as a modern classic. Packed with action from beginning to end, her books are a wild romp through a history that never happened.

THE WOLVES OF WILLOUGHBY CHASE

Even the wolves are not more evil than the cruel Miss Slighcarp . . .

ISBN 0 09 997250 6   £2.99

BLACK HEARTS IN BATTERSEA

Dr Field invited Simon to London – so why can't Simon find him?

ISBN 0 09 988860 2   £3.50

THE CUCKOO TREE

Deadly danger for Dido as she comes up against black magic.

ISBN 0 09 988870 X   £3.50

DIDO AND PA

Why is there a man with a bandaged face hiding in the attic?

ISBN 0 09 988850 5   £3.50

MIDNIGHT IS A PLACE

Thrown out of his home, Lucas must find a way to live in the cruel town of Blastburn.

ISBN 0 09 979200 1   £3.50

Other great reads *from Red Fox*

Paul Zindel is the king of young adult fiction

Sad, but comic and seriously off-the-wall, Paul Zindel's books for young adults are unputdownable.

A STAR FOR THE LATECOMER
with Bonnie Zindel

Brooke's mother would give anything for Brooke to be a star – but her mother's dying.

ISBN 0 09 987200 5 £2.99

A BEGONIA FOR MISS APPLEBAUM

'Miss Applebaum was the most special teacher we ever had . . .'

ISBN 0 09 987210 2 £2.99

THE GIRL WHO WANTED A BOY

Sybella knows more about carburettors than boys – but she wants one, badly.

ISBN 0 09 987180 7 £2.99

THE UNDERTAKER'S GONE BANANAS

No one will believe him but Bobby knows he saw the under-taker strangling his wife.

ISBN 0 09 987190 4 £2.99

PARDON ME, YOU'RE STEPPING ON MY EYEBALL

A tender tale of two mixed-up misfits falling in love.

ISBN 0 09 987220 X £3.50

MY DARLING, MY HAMBURGER

'If a boy gets too pushy,' says Maggie's teacher, 'suggest going for a hamburger.'

ISBN 0 09 987230 7 £3.50

Other great reads from **Red Fox**

Spinechilling stories to read at night

THE CONJUROR'S GAME Catherine Fisher

Alick has unwittingly set something unworldly afoot in Halcombe Great Wood.

ISBN 0 09 985960 2   £2.50

RAVENSGILL William Mayne

What is the dark secret that has held two families apart for so many years?

ISBN 0 09 975270 0   £2.99

EARTHFASTS William Mayne

The bizarre chain of events begins when David and Keith see someone march out of the ground . . .

ISBN 0 09 977600 6   £2.99

A LEGACY OF GHOSTS Colin Dann

Two boys go searching for old Mackie's hoard and find something else . . .

ISBN 0 09 986540 8   £2.99

TUNNEL TERROR

The Channel Tunnel is under threat and only Tom can save it . . .

ISBN 0 09 989030 5   £2.99

Other great reads from *Red Fox*

Superb historical stories from Rosemary Sutcliff

Rosemary Sutcliff tells the historical story better than anyone else. Her tales are of times filled with high adventure, desperate enterprises, bloody encounters and tender romance. Discover the vividly real world of Rosemary Sutcliff today!

THE CAPRICORN BRACELET
ISBN 0 09 977620 0   £2.50

KNIGHT'S FEE
ISBN 0 09 977630 8   £2.99

THE SHINING COMPANY
ISBN 0 09 985580 1   £3.50

THE WITCH'S BRAT
ISBN 0 09 975080 5   £2.50

SUN HORSE, MOON HORSE
ISBN 0 09 979550 7   £2.50

TRISTAN AND ISEULT
ISBN 0 09 979550 7   £2.99

BEOWULF: DRAGON SLAYER
ISBN 0 09 997270 0   £2.50

THE HOUND OF ULSTER
ISBN 0 09 997260 3   £2.99

THE LIGHT BEYOND THE FOREST
ISBN 0 09 997450 9   £2.99

THE SWORD AND THE CIRCLE
ISBN 0 09 997460 6   £2.99